# The Emperor's Tomb

*Also by Joseph Roth*

# The Emperor's Tomb

**JOSEPH ROTH**

Translated by
Michael Hofmann

GRANTA

Granta Publications, 12 Addison Avenue, London W11 4QR
First published in Great Britain by Granta Books, 2013

Originally published in German in 1938 as *Die Kapuzinergruft*

Lines on page vii from *Fado* by Andrzej Stasiuk, translated from the
Polish by Bill Johnston (Dalkey Archive, 2009).

Lines on page vii from 'Refugee Blues' from 'Twelve Songs' in the *Collected Shorter
Poems* 1927–1957 by W. H. Auden (Faber and Faber, 1966).

A CIP catalogue record for this book
is available from the British Library.

1 3 5 7 9 10 8 6 4 2

ISBN 978 1 84708 734 8 (hardback)
ISBN 978 1 84708 612 9 (paperback)

Typeset by M Rules

Printed and bound by CPI Group (UK) Ltd, Croydon, CR0 4YY

# CONTENTS

# TRANSLATOR'S INTRODUCTION

'The homeland, the myth of the homeland, becomes a fundamental value for those who have nothing else.'

Andrzej Stasiuk, *Fado*

'We cannot go there now, my dear, we cannot go there now.'

W. H. Auden, 'Refugee Blues'

*The Emperor's Tomb* – in German *Die Kapuzinergruft*, 'The Crypt of the Capuchins' (the eerie underground burial place of the Habsburgs on the Neuer Markt in the middle of Vienna), and before that variously 'The Cup of Life' and 'A Man Seeks His Fatherland' – was the last novel Joseph Roth wrote, and the last he actually saw in print, in December 1938 or January 1939. *The String of Pearls* was published after his death in May 1939, but was written rather earlier, in 1935 and 1936, only to be overtaken in Roth's gruelling and chaotic final years by this more political and more commercially promising and up-to-the-minute 'sequel' to Roth's most successful novel, *The Radetzky March* of 1932. Both were published (in German) by the tiny Dutch Catholic press, de Gemeenschap, of Bilthoven, Roth having exhausted the few other, more conventional émigré possibilities through a combination of need, under-payment, market-saturation and all-round prickliness.

As a sequel, it is a study in complementarity, but also in contrasts. It is a novel of mothers and marriages where *The Radetzky March* is strictly patrilineal. *The Radetzky March* begins and ends with scenes of battle (Solferino and Krasne-Busk), *The Emperor's Tomb* runs from the eve of one war to the eve of the next, from 1913 to 1938. Where *The Radetzky March* – uniquely in Roth's fiction – impresses with its orchestration, its stateliness, its pageantry, the glorious Tolstoyan fullness of its realization ('done in oils', is how I described it), *The Emperor's Tomb* – the cartoon after the finished painting – seems to revert to Roth's '*Zeitungsroman*' mode of the Twenties, scribbled, spur of the moment, skittish, *distrait*: the numerous short chapters, the insistent tugging at the narrative ('So, in the middle of the summer of 1914, I went to Zlotogrod'), the continual introduction of new characters and locations and abrupt twists and jags in the plot. While the composition of *The Radetzky March* recalls 'broad discs overhanging one another, like the records cued on an old-fashioned gramophone', *The Emperor's Tomb* – colourful, bitty and intense – is more like a shaken kaleidoscope of tumbled glass shards. *The Radetzky March* is wine, *The Emperor's Tomb* – in Yeats's word – 'wine-breath'.

*The Radetzky March* conveys a whole gone world; *The Emperor's Tomb* is more a canny valedictory repertoire of Rothian tropes and characters, done fast, glancingly and sometimes approximately: the spoiled, rather foolish youth; the return to the army; falling in and out of love; male friendships often across gulfs of class, geography and language; the frontier bar; being taken prisoner in the East; the *Heimkehrer* of 1918, who becomes a 'superfluous man' unable to settle into the altered postwar world; a jaundiced view of contemporary design and morals; the centre and the fringes of empire; the operation of treachery and infidelity and economic ruin; the hero's final isolation in space, time and feeling. While *The Radetzky March* can seem like a fabulous concatenation of anthology-ripe scenes never bettered anywhere – seduction, death, duel, feast, drinking, roulette, manoeuvres, battle, you name it – everything in *The Emperor's Tomb* seems to have come from somewhere else in Roth, where it was usually handled with greater expansiveness and willingness. There is something astringent and shorthand and weathered about it. It is a 'slight return', like the 'wheel' of a sestina, or the satyr play concluding a Classical trilogy. It is like one of Elisabeth's blueprints for an unrealized design; a teasing combination of menu and *confit* (in contrast to the opulent multi-course meal that is *Radetzky*). It is laconic and mannerly; spare and drenched in a desperate intensity of feeling; detailed when it wants to be, rapid and fast-forward when it doesn't. (As a measure of this, Roth promised his publishers – with him one almost always wants to say, his poor publishers – a manuscript of 350 pages, but actually delivered just 173.) Where *The Radetzky March* is third person and epic, *The Emperor's Tomb* (though it began in third person) is in a slightly problematical first person. It is not so much a direct sequel, as a sort of round-the-corner continuation, with its three separate moorings: its Trotta is the second cousin of the hero of *The Radetzky March*; its Chojnicki a brother of the wise and far-seeing alchemist count who ends up in the asylum at Steinhof; Onufri and Kapturak are wheeled on again, and its Jacques is a mystical double or perhaps reprise of the original servant character.

Where Austria in *The Radetzky March* is to some extent accidental – it is a great novel about anywhere – *The Emperor's Tomb* is deliberately and unmistakably a book about the Austria of those years, couched between symbol and allegory (what price the lesbian relationship between Elisabeth and Jolanth as a scurrilous reflection of the Dual Monarchy of Austria and Hungary?). It is indeed, as Paul Keegan once put it to me, a 'non-fiction novel', whose characters and action are shaped, if not supplied, by the bigger action of history in those years: sleepwalking into war, defeat, revolution, inflation, confusion of classes (old and new money), Depression, reaction. Most of the characters are weak, but in any case, character is no refuge against such history, any more than a piece of seaweed is against a tide. No one can oppose these developments, no one: not the brilliant violinist Ephraim who gives up his violin for Communist politics and a police bullet; not Elisabeth who goes to Hollywood, nor her father whose brilliant time as a war-profiteer is followed by years of failed and instinctless speculations; not the army bureaucrat Stellmacher, who winds up as an information office on the whereabouts of mostly dead officers; not Joseph Branco whose chestnut-selling tours of the Dual Monarchy are abruptly curtailed by new frontiers; not Frau Trotta who takes refuge in deafness and infirmity, so as not to feel her personal *Anschluss* by the appalling Prussian vulgarian von Stettenheim; and least of all Franz Ferdinand Trotta, awed by his mother but shaped by his father, who does everything that is asked of him, and still winds up alone and in despair. It is no accident that the hero climbs down into the tomb of the Habsburgs, because, in truth, where else is there for him — for Roth — to go in 1938, after the annexation and incorporation of Austria into Hitler's German Reich of March of that year? When the Brownshirt walks into the café at the end to make his pompous announcement, Trotta in his lordly confusion thinks he must have come up out of the toilets, even though part of him knows the toilets are actually elsewhere. Then he thinks the whole world must have been turned upside down, which makes the final descent into the tomb an act of self-preservation as much as one of self-sepulture.

*The Emperor's Tomb* is a strange, wonderful, drastic and unconsoling book. Like *Flight Without End* of 1927, the novel of Roth's it most resembles, it plunges through a world and a lifetime as through a vacuum. The finishing line comes up way before we were ready for it – and we've lost. Was that everything, hero and reader think, in both cases, looking up in startled unison. Well, yes. The haunting final scene of Roth's earlier *Flight Without End* goes – in David Le Vay's translation:

> It was at this hour that my friend Tunda, thirty-two years of age, healthy, and vigorous, a strong young man of diverse talents, stood on the Place de la Madeleine, in the centre of the capital of the world, without any idea what to do. He had no occupation, no desire, no hope, no ambition, and not even any self-love. No one in the whole world was as superfluous as he.

It could almost double as a beginning (indeed, doesn't Musil's *Man Without Qualities* begin similarly, with a city and a gifted man in some perplexity?), only the world is used up and the hero has nothing to offer it. They recoil from each other in mutual disappointment. 'Where can I go now, I, a Trotta?' is a little lower, and a little less clamorous – there is no brass about it, no *thèse*, no *O Welt* outcry – but it's basically the same ending: Tunda the tragedy of potential, Trotta the tragedy of none; Tunda in the capital of the world, Trotta in Germany's newest fiefdom; Tunda on the threshold of a life, Trotta in the house of death. Still, no one who knows both books could fail to be reminded of the other. Indeed, it seems Roth himself was, because at one stage he mailed his publishers the ending for the earlier book. With adorable innocence, they wrote back (16 September 1938):

> It has come to our attention that the last chapter of *The Emperor's Tomb* which you sent us is almost word for word the same as the last chapter of your *Flight Without End*. Is that an error? Surely one can't use exactly the same chapter in two different books.

It's hard to know if Roth purposed anything by it, whether it was a clerical error or an early instance of recycling, or a cynical try-on (all seem possible). There followed some of the usual *Hickhack* – Roth about money, the publishers about the manuscript; then Roth about the manuscript, and the publishers about money – the pages by now had been set! – before, fully two months later, Roth explained that there had indeed been a misunderstanding, and at the eleventh hour the ending of *Flight Without End* was successfully kept out of *The Emperor's Tomb*.

All his life, Roth had an ambivalent attitude to psychology. He was happy to adopt the Freudian picture of the house, with its basement, ground floor, upstairs and attic, but he had no use for Freud's theories or practice. When Stefan Zweig (who wrote a monograph on Freud, spoke at his funeral and counted himself one of his most loyal friends) suggested to Roth that he might be 'subconsciously angry' with him, Roth exploded back (2 April 1936): 'What's that supposed to mean, "subconscious"? It's pure Antichrist!' In *Right and Left* (1929), sounding unusually pompous, Roth proclaims: 'Passions and beliefs are tangled in the minds and hearts of men, and there is no such thing as psychological consistency.' The plurality, the mutability, the essential unknowability of people is one of his great themes. In *The Radetzky March* a woman in the space of a single hour is 'capable of piling the characteristics of all four seasons on a single shoulder'. In *The Leviathan*, Nissen Piczenik has a sudden idea: 'A notion like that arrives suddenly, lightning is slow by comparison, and it hits the very place from where it sprang, which is to say the human heart.' In *Right and Left* again (but of a different character), Roth writes: 'He remembered the lunatic in his village at home, who never tired of asking everyone he met: "How many are you? Are you *one*?" No, one wasn't just *one*. One was ten people, twenty, a hundred. The more opportunities life gave us, the more beings it revealed in us. A man might die because he hadn't experienced anything, and had been just *one* person all his life.' At the same time, it is obvious that Roth is a wonderful observer, an intricate understander and a droll relater of human behaviour. Take, in the present novel, the series of interactions in the third chapter where Trotta acquires his cousin's waistcoat, watch and chain; or, near the end of the book when he realizes how long his mother has been struggling with her deafness; or the time when Jolanth and Elisabeth go to the ladies' loo together, taking care on their way back, to see that they, in their female supremacism, are presented with the bill, and not Trotta. All this is nothing if not psychology, but psychology of an unusual sort, namely something momentary and dramatic, on occasion even catastrophic. It is a thunderbolt or lightning-flash, not a climate to be measured, calculated and predicted – something you might take an umbrella for, or a sweater-vest. Consistency doesn't interest Roth,* perhaps even at a certain level, plausibility; and if plausibility, then as a servant not as a master. What interests him is change.

In an odd way, *The Emperor's Tomb* is a sort of *Bildungsroman*, beginning with a privileged, rather shallow character (technically an adult though he continues to see himself primarily as a child), and ending with a Lear-like figure, with nothing but the first stirrings of wisdom and dignity. To do this, Roth has had to deepen the character as he went along: begin with one of his trustful blockheads (I don't think I'm exaggerating), and end not just with experience and pain, but grafting on a nervous system and an intelligence with which to absorb them. Austria, the culture of *Sachertorten* and Sacher-Masoch and whipped cream and Klimt and Strauss and braided uniforms and archaic usages and Schnitzler and sweet little girls in the sticks (of the name of a girl in a *Trafik* scrawled on a box of cigarettes – a name, incidentally, almost identical to that of Roth's poor schizophrenic wife, Friedl Reichler) needed to be made into a subject for tragedy, because that was how Roth understood what had happened to

---

* Perhaps this is the place to draw the reader's attention to a handful of minor inconsistencies in the text, which I have of course let stand: a little toing and froing in the months around the beginning of World War One; a little wavering in the names of the cafés; and the fact that the doors to Jadlowker's border tavern are 'grass-green' in one place and later 'brown', and that Jacques is described now as having hair, now as bald. *Honi soit.*

it, and he was no longer interested in writing anything else. Hence – I imagine – the switch during the writing of the novel from third person to first. Roth wanted access to his own intelligence and anguish and dignity. He therefore had to merge or morph his hero with himself, and he could only do it with the discretion afforded by the first person. (The book moves, you might say, from Trotta in the morning to Roth at night. The one who is woken up in the morning is not the same as the other who can't go to bed at night. It's only when you put it down at the end that you realize that something has happened to our hero or anti-hero.) Trotta has gone along rather purposelessly, except for, in his rather baffled and passive way, accruing losses – except for (as we say) de-accessioning. In the space of not many pages, he has lost basically everything: his mother, their servant, his wife, his child, his house, his cousin and his Jewish friend, his noble friends and his Polish Siberian friend, the remains of his fortune, even the quality of the night in Vienna at the turn of the century. The ending is naked self-portraiture. It is not the property of a character in a fictional situation, but the feeling Roth gives voice to *in propria persona* in his non-fiction of the time, the atmosphere of terminal dereliction and hopelessness experienced and expressed in pieces like 'In the Bistro After Midnight'(November 1938) or 'Rest While Watching the Demolition' (June 1938):

When the first silvery streetlights glimmer on, a refugee, an exile, sometimes comes along, without a wanderer's staff, quite as if he were at home here, and – as if he wanted to prove to me in one breath that he felt at home, that he knew his way around, but also that where he felt at home wasn't home — he says: 'I know somewhere you can get a good, cheap meal here.' And I'm glad for him that he does. I'm glad that he walks off under the trail of silvery streetlights, and doesn't stop, now that night is falling, to take in the ever-ghostlier-looking dust on the empty lot opposite. Not everyone has to get used to rubble and to shattered walls.

The exile, the displaced person, has taken the newspapers away with him. He wants to read them in his good, cheap restaurant. In front of me the table is empty.

'Where can I go now, I, a Trotta?' is absolutely of a piece with that terminal desolation — not least as 'Trotta' chimes with the German '*Toter*', a dead man.

In Roth, the practical and the quixotic are usually inextricable and inseparable. In February 1938, he visited Vienna for the last time, *mirabile dictu,* on a diplomatic mission for the Habsburg Legitimists; he spoke on behalf of the young Otto von Habsburg (grandson of Franz Joseph, and Pretendant to the throne that had been abolished at Versailles in 1918) to members of the Austrian government. He got a dusty answer and will have sensed the atmosphere himself (like Trotta's friends suddenly melting away from the café table where they had all been sitting a moment before). A month later, huge crowds turned out to greet Hitler and the Wehrmacht. After a life spent for the most part in exile, and in the service of European unity,

Otto von Habsburg died on 4 July 2011 at the age of ninety-eight, and was buried in the *Kapuzinergruft*, where Joseph Roth, one of his last and least and unlikeliest and so to speak ferventest subjects ended his last novel seventy years – *ein Menschenalter*, a biblical lifetime – before. The one word on his tomb (I seem to remember hearing late one night on the BBC World Service) is *Frieden* – Peace.

Michael Hofmann
August 2012

# I

We are the Trottas. My people's roots are in Sipolje, in Slovenia. I say 'people' because we're not a family any more. Sipolje no longer exists, hasn't for a long time. It's been assimilated with several other villages to form a middle-sized town. As everyone knows, that's the trend nowadays. People are no longer capable of staying on their own. They form into nonsensical groups, and it's the same way with the villages. Nonsensical structures come into being. The farmers move into the cities, and the villages themselves – they want to be cities.

I remember Sipolje from when I was a boy. My father took me there once, on 17 August, the eve of the day when all over the country, even in the smallest hamlets, they used to celebrate the birthday of Emperor Franz Joseph. In modern Austria, and in the former Crown Lands, there are probably only a handful of people to whom our name means anything. Where you will find our name, though, is in the lost annals of the former

Austro-Hungarian army, and I will admit I'm proud of the fact – especially because the annals are lost. I am not a child of these particular times; in fact I find it difficult not to declare myself their enemy. Not because I don't understand them, as I like to claim. That's my excuse. The fact is that manners don't allow me to be unpleasant or aggressive and so I say I don't understand something, when really I ought to say I hate it or despise it. My hearing is acute, so I pretend to be a little deaf. To me it seems better breeding to feign an infirmity than to admit I've heard an unpleasant sound.

My grandfather's brother was the infantry lieutenant who saved the life of Emperor Franz Joseph at the battle of Solferino. The lieutenant was ennobled. For a long time afterwards he was known as the Hero of Solferino, in the army and in the reading primers of the Dual Monarchy, until, in accordance with his own wishes, the shadow of oblivion settled over him. He took his leave. He is buried in Hietzing. On his gravestone are the quiet, defiant words: 'Here lies the Hero of Solferino.'

The Imperial grace and favour were extended to his son, who became District Commissioner, and to his grandson, who fell in autumn 1914 at the battle of Krasne-Busk as a lieutenant of the Jägers. I never met him, as indeed I never met any of the ennobled branch of our people. The ennobled Trottas were all loyal servants to Franz Joseph. My father, though, was a rebel.

My father was a rebel and a patriot of a sort that only existed in the old Austria-Hungary. He wanted to reform the Empire and save the Habsburgs. His understanding of the Dual Monarchy was too acute. He therefore aroused suspicion, and was forced to emigrate. As a young man still, he went to America. He became a chemical engineer. In those days they needed people like him in the sprawling dye works of New York and Chicago. When he was still poor, the only sort of homesickness he felt was for the countryside. But once he had made his fortune, he started to feel homesick for Austria. He came home. He settled in Vienna. He had money, and the Austrian police liked people with money. My father was not merely left alone. He was permitted to found a new Slovene party, and bought a couple of newspapers in Zagreb.

He made some influential friends in the circle of the heir to the throne, Archduke Franz Ferdinand. My father dreamed of a Slavic kingdom under the overall suzerainty of the Habsburgs. He dreamed, if you will, of a Triple Monarchy. And perhaps it is only right for me, his son, to say I like to think that if my father had been spared, he might have changed the course of history. But he died, some eighteen months before Franz Ferdinand was murdered. I am his only son. In his will he bequeathed me his ideas. Not for nothing did he have me christened Franz Ferdinand. But I was young and foolish then, not to say frivolous. I was certainly frivolous as well. I lived, as they say, into the day. No! That's wrong. I lived into the night; the days were for sleeping.

# II

Early one morning – it was in April of 1914, and I was still groggy, having gone to bed only one or two hours before – a visitor was announced, a cousin of mine, by the name of Trotta.

In my dressing gown and slippers I padded out to the antechamber. The windows were open wide. The morning blackbirds in our garden were warbling away. The early sun merrily poured into the room. Our maid, whom I had never seen so early in the day before, looked unfamiliar to me in her blue apron – I only knew her in her formal evening incarnation, assembled from blond, black and white, something like a flag. It was the first time I had seen her in her blue gear, which resembled the sort of thing that engineers and gasmen wear, wielding a purple feather duster – the sight of her alone would have been enough to change my ideas about life. For the first time in years I beheld the morning in my house, and I saw that it was beautiful. I liked the maid. I liked the open windows. I liked the sun. I liked the singing of the blackbirds. It was as golden as the morning sun. Even the girl in her blue outfit was somehow as golden as the sun. There was so much gold about that at first I failed to make out the visitor who was waiting for me. I only noticed him a couple of seconds – or perhaps minutes – later. Lean, swarthy and silent, he was sitting in the only chair our anteroom had to offer, and he didn't budge when I entered. Even with his black hair and moustache, and his brown skin, he too amidst the matutinal gold of the anteroom was like a piece of the sun, albeit some distant southern sun. He reminded me spontaneously of my late father. He too had been dark and lean, bony and brown, swarthy and a real child of the sun, not like us, its fair-haired stepchildren. I speak Slovene, my father had taught me. I greeted my Trotta cousin in his native tongue. It seemed not to surprise him. What else was I going to do? He didn't get up, he remained seated. He held out his hand to me. He smiled. His big strong teeth gleamed under his blue-black moustache. He said 'Du' to me right away. I felt: he's not a cousin, he's my brother! He had my address from the lawyer. 'Your father', he began, 'left me 2000 gulden in his will, and I have come to collect them. I want to thank you. Tomorrow I will go home. I have a sister, who will be able to get married now. With a dowry of 500 gulden, she will get the richest farmer in Sipolje.'

'What about the rest of the money?'

'That's for me,' he said serenely. He smiled, and it seemed to me the sun was pouring into our anteroom even more brightly.

'What will you do with the money?'

'I will invest it in my business,' he replied. And as though the moment to introduce himself had finally come, he got up from his chair, there was a confident swagger as he stood there, and a touching formality with which he introduced himself. 'Joseph Branco's the name,' he said. Only then did I remember I was standing in front of my visitor in dressing-gown and slippers. I asked him to wait, and went back into my room to dress.

# III

It was no later than seven o'clock when we strolled into the Café Magerl. The first of the baker's delivery boys were just arriving, snow white and smelling of crisp rolls and poppy seed biscuits and salt sticks. The day's first freshly roasted coffee, virginal and spicy, smelled like a morning within a morning. My cousin Joseph Branco was sitting beside me, swarthy and southern, merry, healthy and alert. I felt ashamed of my haggardness and my almost colourless pallor. I was a little uncomfortable as well. What was I going to talk to him about? It made me a little more uncomfortable when he said: 'I don't drink coffee in the morning. I want soup.' Of course. In Sipolje the peasants started the day with potato soup.

So I ordered potato soup for him. It was a long time coming, and in the meantime I was bashfully dipping my almond croissant in my coffee. Finally it did come, a steaming bowlful. My cousin Joseph Branco disregarded his spoon. He raised the steaming bowl to his mouth in his black-haired brown hands. While he drank his soup, he seemed to have forgotten about me. Completely concentrating on his steaming bowl, supported on the tips of his strong, slim fingers, he looked like a person in whom appetite is a noble thing, and who disdained a spoon because it is nobler to drink straight from the bowl. Yes, while I watched him drinking his soup, I was almost perplexed by the fact that people had bothered to invent something as ridiculous as spoons. My cousin set down his bowl, and I could see that it was smooth and empty and clean as if it had just been wiped and washed.

'This afternoon', he said, 'I will collect the money.' What sort of business was it, I asked him, that he was planning to invest in. 'Oh,' he said, 'a very small business, but something that will keep a man fed through the winter.'

And so I learned that in spring, summer and autumn my cousin Joseph Branco was a farmer, tending his fields, but in winter he was a chestnut-roaster. He had a sheepskin, a mule, a small cart, a roasting-pan and five sacks of chestnuts. Thus equipped, he set off every year at the beginning of November through some of the Monarchy's Crown Lands. If he happened to like it in one particular place, he would spend the whole winter there until the storks came. Then he would tie the empty sacks round the mule and go to the nearest railway station. He put the mule in a cattle car, boarded the train, went home and became a farmer again.

I asked him how it was possible to expand such a small business, and he indicated there were various possibilities. For instance, one might offer a sideline in baked apples and baked potatoes, in addition to the chestnuts. Also, his mule was old and feeble, and it was almost time to buy a new one. He had a couple of hundred crowns already saved up.

He wore a shimmering satin jacket, a flowery velvet waistcoat with coloured-glass buttons and a heavy, braided gold watch chain looped round his neck. And I, who had been raised by my father to love the Slavs of our Empire, and who was therefore apt to take any sort of folkloric detail for a totem, straightaway fell for the chain. I wanted to have it. I asked my cousin how much it cost. 'I don't know,' he said. 'I got it from my father, and he got it from his father, it's not the sort of thing you can buy. But seeing as you're my cousin, I'll sell it to you.' 'How much is it, then?' I asked. And there I was, mindful of everything my father had inculcated into me, thinking to myself that a Slovene farmer is far too noble to think of money and prices. My cousin Joseph Branco thought for a long time, and finally he said: 'Twenty-three crowns.' I didn't ask how he arrived at this particular figure. I gave him twenty-five. He counted them out, made no move to give me two crowns' change, pulled out a great red-and-blue checked handkerchief, and wrapped the money in that. Only then, after twice knotting the handkerchief, did he take off the chain, pull the watch out of his waistcoat pocket, and lay watch and chain on the table. It was an old-fashioned heavy silver watch, with a little key to wind it. My cousin seemed a little reluctant to detach it from the chain, looked at it tenderly, almost devoutly, for a long time, and finally said, 'Well, seeing as you're my cousin! If you give me another three crowns, you can have the watch as well!' I gave him a whole five-crown piece. He didn't give me any change this time either. Once again, he produced his handkerchief, unpicked the double knot, put the new coin in with the other money, stuffed the handkerchief back in his pocket and looked at me with his big brown eyes.

'I like your waistcoat too!' I said after an interval of a few seconds. 'I'll buy that off you as well.'

'Because you're my cousin,' he replied, 'I'll sell you my waistcoat as well.' And, not hesitating for a moment, he pulled off his jacket, took off his waistcoat and passed it across the table to me. 'It's good material,' said Joseph Branco, 'and the buttons are pretty. Because it's you, I'll only ask two fifty.' I gave him three crowns, and in his eyes I could clearly see disappointment that it wasn't five again. He seemed disgruntled, stopped smiling, but in the end he stowed the money away just as carefully and elaborately as he had done with the rest.

So now I had, as I saw it, the most important attributes of a proper Slovene: an old watch-chain, a brightly coloured waistcoat and a heavy lump of a watch, stopped, with a key to wind it. I didn't hesitate. I put on all three items on the spot, paid, and ordered up a fiacre. I accompanied my cousin to his hotel; he was staying at the Green Huntsman. I asked him to wait for me tonight, so that I could collect him. I wanted to introduce him to my friends.

## IV

For form's sake, and to calm my anxious mother, I was enrolled as a student of laws. I did no studying. All of life lay spread out in front of me like a flowery meadow, barely confined by the rim of a very, very distant horizon. I lived in the merry, even uproarious society of young aristocrats, the class that, along with artists, I liked best in the old Empire. I shared their sceptical frivolity, their resourceful melancholy, their sinful negligence, their proud sense of doom – all of them signs of the end which we failed to see coming. Over the glasses from which we drank to excess, an invisible Death was already crossing his bony hands. We chuntered away, we even blasphemed mindlessly. Alone and old, almost petrified in his remoteness, but still close to us and ubiquitous in the great and colourful Empire lived and ruled the old Emperor Franz Joseph. It was possible that in the misty depths of our souls there slumbered those certainties called instincts, the certainty above all that with each passing day the old Emperor was dying, and with him the monarchy, not so much a fatherland as an empire, something greater, wider, more spacious and all-encompassing than just a fatherland. From out of our heavy hearts there bubbled forth the light witticisms, from our sense of doom a foolish pleasure in every affirmation of life: in balls, in Heurigen wine taverns, in girls, in food, in coach rides and follies of all sorts, in silly japes and suicidal ironies, vehemence and outspokenness, in the Prater, in the big wheel and puppet shows, in masquerade balls and ballets, in risky flirtations in the silent boxes of the Hofoper, in manoeuvres we slept through and even in those infections we sometimes caught from love.

The reader will understand that the unexpected arrival of my cousin was welcome to me. None of my frivolous friends could boast of a cousin like that, a waistcoat like that, a watch-chain like that, such a close tie to the semi-mythical soil of the Slovene village of Sipolje, the home of the then not yet forgotten, but already legendary Hero of Solferino.

In the evening, I collected my cousin. His shining satin jacket made a great impression on all my friends. He babbled away in an incomprehensible German, laughed a lot with his strong white teeth, allowed us all to buy him drinks, promised to kit out my friends with new waistcoats and watch-chains from Slovenia, and was happy to accept down-payments. Everyone envied me my waistcoat, watch and chain. If they could, they would have happily bought my whole cousin off me, my relations and my Sipolje.

My cousin promised to be back in the autumn. We all

trooped off to the station. I bought him a second-class ticket. He took it to the ticket office, and managed to swap it for a third-class one. Then he proceeded to wave to us. We were all heartbroken when the train rumbled out of the station; because we were as prone to melancholy as we were avid for pleasure.

# V

We went on talking about my cousin Joseph Branco for at least another day or two. Then we forgot about him again, or, if you like, we set him aside for the time being. Because we had other, more current follies that wanted to be aired and celebrated.

It wasn't until late summer, on or about 20 August, that I received a letter from Joseph Branco, written in Slovene, which that same evening I translated to my friends. It described the Veterans' Association's celebration of the Emperor's birthday in Sipolje. Branco himself was a reservist; he was still too young to belong to the Association. Even so, he marched with them to the forest clearing where they held a big party every 18th August, simply because none of the oldsters was up to carrying the big side drum. There were five brass players and three clarinettists. But what good is a marching band without a big side drum?

'I don't understand those peculiar Slovenes,' said young Festetics. 'The Hungarians rob them of their most basic national rights, and they retaliate, they even rebel, or it looks like they might rebel, and then they go and celebrate the King's birthday.'

'There's nothing peculiar about the Monarchy,' replied Count Chojnicki, the oldest of our group. 'But for our moronic government' (he was given to strong expressions), 'nothing would look at all out of the way. By which I mean that so far as Austria-Hungary is concerned, the ostensibly peculiar is perfectly natural. It's only in this crazy Europe of nation-states and nationalists that the natural looks peculiar. Of course it's the Slovenes and Poles and the Ruthenian Galicians, and the kaftan Jews from Boryslaw, the horse-dealers from Bačka, the Moslems from Sarajevo and the chestnut roasters from Mostar who sing the "*Gott erhalte*". While the German students from Brünn and Eger, the dentists, apothecaries, hairdressers' apprentices, photographers from Linz, Graz, Knittelfeld, the goitres from the Alpine valleys, they all sing the "*Wacht am Rhein*". Gentlemen, I predict that Austria will be destroyed by that Nibelung tendency! The heart of Austria is not the centre, but the periphery. You won't find Austria in the Alps – chamois, yes, and edelweiss and gentians but barely a hint of the double-headed eagle. The substance of Austria is drawn and replenished from the Crown Lands.'

Baron Kovacs, recent military nobility of Hungarian descent, screwed in his monocle, as was his wont when he thought he had something especially important to say. He spoke in the harsh and melodious German of the Magyars, not so much out of necessity as from a dissenter's pride. As he did, his crumpled face that looked like dough that has failed to rise flushed violently. 'It is the Hungarians who have most to suffer in this Double Monarchy,' he said. It was his statement of faith; the words might have been graven in bronze. He bored all of us and he infuriated Chojnicki, the oldest and most highly strung of our little group. Chojnicki's standard riposte inevitably followed. As ever, he recited: 'The Hungarians, my dear Kovacs, are responsible for oppressing the following peoples: the Slovaks, Romanians, Croats, Serbs, Ruthenians, Bosnians, the Swabians of the Bačka, and the Saxons of Timisoara.' He counted them on the spread fingers of his fine, strong, slender hands.

Kovacs laid his monocle on the table. Chojnicki's words seemed to have made no impression on him. I know what I know, he thought, as he always did. Sometimes he said it aloud too.

He was a harmless, on occasion even a good young man; I couldn't bear him. Even so, I strove to generate a friendly feeling for him. I suffered because I didn't like him, and for a reason: I was in love with his sister. Her name was Elisabeth, and she was all of nineteen.

I'd been fighting against the feeling for a long time in vain, not so much because I felt at risk, but because I dreaded the silent mockery of my cynical friends. Back then, before the Great War, the fashion was for arrogance and cynicism, a silly genuflection to the so-called '*décadence*', a lassitude that was half-affected and half-genuine, and a groundless boredom. This was the atmosphere in which I spent my best years. It was an atmos-

phere that had little use for emotions, while passion was positively scorned. My friends had inconsequential little 'liaisons,'
women you set aside and occasionally loaned out like macs;
women you accidentally forgot, like umbrellas, or on purpose,
like boring parcels you didn't go back for, for fear of being re-
attached to them. In the circles in which I moved love was
accounted an aberration, an engagement was like an apoplexy,
and a marriage something like a long illness. We were young.
We accepted that sometime in the course of our lives we would
probably get married, but we felt similarly about the arterial
sclerosis that would probably befall us in twenty or thirty years
as well. I had numerous opportunities for being alone with the
girl, though at that time it was by no means accepted that young
ladies could consort with young gentlemen for longer than an
hour without some fitting, positively legitimate pretext. I only
took advantage of a handful of such opportunities. As I say, I
would have been ashamed to use all of them, because of my
friends. Yes, I was scrupulously careful that my feeling didn't
show, and I was often worried that someone or other in my
circle might have got wind of it, because of some indiscretion
of mine. When I ran into my friends unexpectedly from time
to time, their sudden silence left me convinced that they had
just been talking about my love of Elisabeth Kovacs, and I felt
all glum about it, as though I'd been caught doing something
bad, as though some nasty, despicable weakness had been discovered in me. But during the few hours I spent alone with
Elisabeth, I thought I could feel how shallow and unworthy the
mockery of my friends was, their cynicism and their affected

'*décadence*'. At the same time, however, I felt a little guilty too, as though I had betrayed their high and holy principles. In a way I was leading a kind of double life, and I didn't feel very good about it.

At that time, Elisabeth was beautiful, soft, tender, and unquestionably devoted to me. The smallest, the least of her actions and gestures moved me deeply, because I felt that every movement of her hand, every nod of her head, every swing of her foot, the smoothing of her skirt, the gentle raising of her veil, the touch of her lip on a cup of coffee, a particular flower in her corsage, the way she pulled off a glove, all carried a clear and immediate message for me – and for me alone. Yes, from various signs that might then have been accounted 'forward', I thought I was entitled to conclude that the tenderness with which she eyed me, an impetuous or ostensibly accidental touch on my hand or my shoulder were in the nature of binding promises of great and delicious tendernesses to come, if I liked. The eves of celebrations whose calendrical certainty was beyond questioning. Her voice was low and soft (I dislike shrill soprano voices). Her speaking put me in mind of a stifled, tamed, chaste and yet suggestive cooing, the purling of underground streams, the rumbling of distant trains that one sometimes hears on sleepless nights, and each of her words, however trite, because of the timbre of her speech, acquired the portentousness and gravitas of some far-off, maybe not readily understandable, but clearly intuited lost ur-language once maybe heard in dreams.

When I left her to return to the society of my friends, I felt tempted to tell them all about Elisabeth, yes, even to rave to them about her. But at the sight of their tired, slack and cynical faces, their palpable and even obtrusive mockery, that I not only didn't care to have levelled at me, but was keen to participate in as a regular contributor, I first lapsed into a dull and sheepish silence, and then, within a few minutes, fell in with that arrogant '*décadence*' whose lost and proud sons we all were.

Such was my foolish cleft stick, and I honestly didn't know where to find comfort. I occasionally thought about taking my mother into my confidence. But at that time, while I was still young, I thought her incapable of understanding my concerns. My relationship with my mother was not honest and authentic, but rather the pathetic effort to imitate those that my friends had with their mothers. To them, they weren't mothers, but a sort of hatchery to which they owed life and maturity, or, at best, a sort of domestic setting in which they happened to have come into the world, and to which they owed nothing more than a respectful acknowledgment. I, though, felt an almost holy awe for my mother all my life; only I chose to suppress it. I ate lunch at home. We sat silently opposite each other at the big table in the spacious dining room. My father's old place at the head of the table was kept vacant, and every day in accordance with my mother's wishes, a setting was put out for the permanent absentee. You could say my mother sat at the right hand of the departed, and I on his left. She drank a golden muscadet, and I a half bottle of Vöslauer. (I didn't like it. I would have preferred Burgundy. But my mother had decreed it so.) Our old servant

Jacques waited on us, with his trembling old man's hands in snow-white gloves. His thick hair was almost equally white. My mother ate small portions, quickly but with dignity. As soon as I raised my eyes to her, she lowered hers to her plate – even though just a moment before, I had sensed her looking at me. Oh, I could feel that she had many things she wanted to ask me, and only bit them back to save herself the shame of being lied to by her only child. She carefully folded up her napkin. Those were the only moments I could look closely at her broad, slightly puffy face, with the slack cheeks, and the creased heavy lids. I looked down at her lap where she was folding the napkin, and I thought reverently but also reproachfully that it was from there that my life had taken its inception, that warm lap, the most motherly part of my mother, and I felt some astonishment that I could sit there so silently, so truculently, yes, so obtusely, and that she, my own mother, could find no words to say to me, and that obviously she felt just as ashamed of her grown-up, too rapidly grown up son, as I did of her, my aged, too rapidly aged progenetrix. How I wished I could have been able to talk to her about my cleft stick, my double life between Elisabeth and my friends. But she clearly didn't want to hear anything of what she sensed, so as not to have to condemn aloud what she disapproved of in quiet. Perhaps, probably in fact, she had come to terms with the terrible law of nature that compels sons quickly to forget their origins; to see their mothers as old ladies; no longer to think of the breasts at which they first sucked – an unyielding law, that also compels the mothers to see the fruit of their womb grow bigger and taller and stranger and more remote; initially with pain, then with bitterness, and finally with resignation. I felt my mother spoke to me so little because she didn't want me to say things for which she would have had to chide me. But if I had felt myself at liberty to talk with her about Elisabeth, and my love for that girl, then I would probably have dishonoured her, my mother, and so to speak myself as well. Sometimes I did want to talk about my love. But then I thought about my friends. Their relationships with their mothers. I had the childlike feeling that by confessing I would betray myself. As if keeping silent about something to my mother wasn't a betrayal of myself, and moreover a betrayal of my mother. When my friends spoke about their mothers, I felt triply ashamed: for my friends, my mother, and myself. They spoke of their mothers almost the way they spoke of their 'liaisons' that they had stood up or left behind, as if they were prematurely aged mistresses, and worse, as if the mothers were undeserving of such sons.

So it was my friends who kept me from hearing the voice of nature and common sense, and from giving free expression either to my feeling for my dear Elisabeth or to my filial love of my mother.

But it was to become apparent that the sins with which my friends and I burdened our souls were not personal to ourselves, but only the feeble, barely discernible signs of the coming devastation I will tell you about shortly.

# VI

Before the great devastation began, it was given to me to meet the Jew Manes Reisiger, who has a part to play in this story later. He came from Zlotogrod in Galicia. A little later, I got to see Zlotogrod for myself, so I can describe it to you here. It matters to me so much because it no longer exists, no more than Sipolje does. It was destroyed in the course of the war. It used to be a town once: a small town, but still a town. Today it is an expanse of meadow. Clover grows there in the summer, crickets shrill in the tall grasses, earthworms thrive in plump coils, and the larks come with jabbing beaks to gobble them up.

The Jew Manes Reisiger came to see me one day in October, just as early in the morning as his friend, my cousin Branco, had come to see me a couple of months before. He came, in fact, on the recommendation of my cousin Branco. 'Young master' – thus Jacques – 'a Jew would like to speak to you.' I knew a few Jews at the time, Viennese Jews admittedly. I didn't hate them

22

by any means, because at that time the virulent anti-Semitism of the nobility and the circles in which I moved had become fashionable with janitors, with the lower middle classes, with chimneysweeps and house painters. This change reflected the democratizing drift of fashion, whereby the daughter of a court usher wore exactly the same veil on her Sunday hat as a Trautmannsdorf or a Szechenyi had worn three years before, on a weekday. And just as no Szechenyi could possibly wear the same veil that graced the hat of an usher's daughter, so the high society of which I counted myself a member could not possibly turn up their noses at a Jew – simply because my janitor already did.

I stepped into the anteroom, prepared to see one of those Jews I knew, whose profession seemed to have affected, even to have become, their physical aspect. I knew money-changers, pedlars, garment-dealers and brothel pianists. Stepping into the anteroom, I beheld a man who not only failed to correspond to my notions of a Jew, but who might have been enough all on his own to demolish them. He was incredibly dark and incredibly big. It would be incorrect to say that his beard, his sleek, deep black beard framed his tough, tanned, bony face. No, it was the face that emerged from the beard, as though the beard had been there first, before the face, and had spent years waiting for something to frame and surround. The man was big and strong. In his hand he held a peaked corduroy cap, and on his head he wore a round velvet kippah, of the sort our clerics sometimes wear. He stood in the doorway, mighty, sinister, a force of nature, his red hands clenched into fists, hanging like two hammers from the black sleeves of his kaftan. Out of the leather lining of his cap he took a multiply folded letter in Slovene from my cousin Joseph Branco. I asked him to sit down, but he motioned that he wouldn't, and the gesture struck me as even more bashful than it was already because it had been performed by those hands, either one of which would have been enough to crush me, the window, the little marble table, the clothes stand and everything else that was in the anteroom. I read the letter. It informed me that the man standing before me was Manes Reisiger from Zlotogrod, coachman by trade, friend of my cousin Joseph Branco, who, on his annual transits through the Crown Lands of the Monarchy to sell chestnuts, enjoyed free board and lodging with the bearer of the letter, Manes Reisiger, and that the ties of friendship and family obliged me to do all I could to help the said Manes Reisiger.

And what help did he want, Manes Reisiger from Zlotogrod?

Nothing more and nothing less than a free place at the conservatory for his gifted son, Ephraim. He was not to become a coachman like his father, and not to go to seed in the Eastern marches of the monarchy. According to his father, Ephraim was a prodigy.

I promised. I set off to visit my friend, Count Chojnicki, first because he was the only Galician among my friends, and second because he was the only one who was capable of breaking the ancient, traditional, invariable and insidiously effective resistance of Austrian officialdom: by threats, by force, by subtlety and deception, the weapons of an old culture: the weapons of our world.

That evening, I saw Count Chojnicki in our café, which was the Café Wimmerl.

I knew that one could hardly please him more than by turning to him for a favour for one of his countrymen. Chojnicki had neither job nor occupation. He, who could have made a so-called brilliant career in the army, in the government, in the diplomatic service, and who had disdained such a thing for contempt of the fools, the imbeciles, the eejits who ran the state, took a keen delight in making Court Councillors aware of his power, which was a real power, conferred upon him by standing outside all hierarchies. And he, who was so kindly and so gracious to waiters, coachmen, constables and postmen, who never forgot to doff his hat when asking a policeman or porter for directions, was barely recognizable when he undertook one of his protection errands to the Ballhausplatz, the Statthalterei or the Ministry of Culture and Education: an icy loftiness lay over his features like a transparent visor. If he had shown himself to be agreeable, even affable, to the liveried doorman at the gate, then his aversion to officialdom seemed to grow with every step he climbed, until by the time he had reached the top floor, he looked every inch a man who had come to hold some fearsome inquest. In the ministries he was a well-known figure. And when, in his dangerously quiet voice, he told the aide in the corridor: Announce me to the Court Councillor!, it rarely happened that he was asked for his name, and if he was, then he merely said again, if anything more quietly still: Kindly announce me right away! Perhaps the word 'kindly' was spoken a little louder.

Moreover, he adored music, and for that reason too it seemed appropriate to try and enlist his support for young Reisiger. With typical impulsiveness, he promised to go the very next day. His alacrity was such that I felt a little conscience-stricken, and asked him if he didn't require some proof of young Reisiger's talent before going to do battle on his behalf. That merely irritated him. 'You may know your Slovenes,' he said, 'but I know my Galician Jews. The father's name is Manes, you tell me, and he's a coachman. The son's name is Ephraim, and that's all I need to know. I am utterly convinced of the gifts of the young man. I trust my instincts. My Galician Jews can do anything. Only ten years ago I didn't much care for them. Now I love them dearly because all those eejits are anti-Semites now. I need only inquire who is serving in the relevant department, and who among them is the most outspoken anti-Semite. Then I will flaunt my little Ephraim at him, and I will go in the company of his father as well. I hope he looks thoroughly Jewish.'

'He wears a kaftan,' I began. 'Perfect,' exclaimed Count Chojnicki, 'then he's my man. You know, I'm no patriot, but I love my countrymen. A country, a fatherland, there's something abstract about that. But a countryman is something concrete. I can't possibly love every wheat and maize field, every pine forest, every swamp, every Polish lady and gentleman, but show me one field, one copse, one swamp, one individual, well, *à la bonheur*! That's something I can see and understand, that speaks to me in a language I am familiar with, that – because of its singularity – can be dear to me. And beyond that, there are persons I term my countrymen, even if they happen to have been born in China or Persia or Africa. Some are dear to me from the moment I first clap eyes on them. A true 'countryman' is immediately identifiable. And if he happens to be someone from my own patch as well, then, as I say, *à la bonheur*! But there's an element of chance there, the other is simple providence.' He raised his glass, and called out: 'Here's to my countrymen, wherever they happen to hail from!'

Two days later, I brought along the coachman Manes Reisiger to see him in the Hotel Kremser. Manes perched on the edge of his chair, not moving, a dark colossus. He appeared not to have sat down himself, but to have been placed there rather approximately by some agency, and as though he wouldn't allow himself to occupy the whole of a chair. Aside from a couple of sentences he repeated at intervals for no very good reason – namely, 'Please, gentlemen!' and 'Thank you, kind sirs!' – he said nothing, nor did he seem to follow the proceedings very closely. It was Chojnicki who was giving the coachman Manes from Zlotogrod a lecture on all things Zlotogrod; for Chojnicki was very well acquainted with all parts of Galicia.

'Well then, tomorrow at eleven, we'll go and sort out your affair,' he said.

'Thank you, kind sirs!' said Manes. In one hand he waved his peaked corduroy cap, and with the other he doffed his kippah. He bowed once more at the door that the porter held open for him, and to whom he shot a grateful and happy smile.

A couple of weeks later, young Ephraim Reisiger had his place in the conservatory. The boy came to Chojnicki to thank him. I happened to be present in Chojnicki's hotel. Young

Ephraim Reisiger almost scowled, and all the while he was expressing his gratitude, he looked more like a youth who is bringing a complaint. He spoke Polish, of which, thanks to my Slovene, I understood roughly every third word. But the mien of Count Chojnicki gave me to understand that the surly and basically ungrateful attitude of the boy pleased him.

'Isn't that something!' he said, once the boy had left. 'Our people don't say thank you – more the opposite. They are proud people, the Galician Jews – my Galician Jews! They live in the belief that distinctions are theirs as of right. They respond to grace and favour with the same wonderful equanimity with which they receive abuse and stones. All other people wax indignant when they are abused, and bow and scrape when they receive a favour. My Polish Jews are equally immune to abuse and to kindness. In their own way, they are aristocrats. For the mark of an aristocrat above all is equanimity; and never have I seen greater equanimity than in my Polish Jews!'

My Polish Jews, he said, in the same tone as he had so often spoken to me of 'my estates', 'my Impressionists', 'my musical instrument collection'. I had a distinct sense that part of the reason he so admired the Jews was that he saw them as his property. It was as though they hadn't seen the light of the world in Galicia because of God's will, but because he personally had ordered them from the Almighty, just as he ordered Persian carpets from the noted seller Pollitzer, and parrots from the Italian birdseller Scapini, and rare old musical instruments from the violin maker Grossauer. And with the same attention to detail, the same circumspect nobility with which he treated his carpets and birds and instruments, so he encountered his Jews, so that he took it for his self-evident duty to write the good coachman Manes, the father of that arrogant boy, a letter congratulating him on Ephraim's acceptance in the conservatory. Chojnicki was afraid the coachman Manes might thank him first.

But the coachman Manes Reisiger, far from writing a letter of thanks, and wholly unable to see the smile of fortune that had brought him and his son into the proximity of Count Chojnicki and myself, rather assuming that his son Ephraim was so inordinately talented that a Viennese conservatory must count itself lucky to have someone like his son, visited me two days later, and began as follows: 'If anyone can do anything in this world, then it is my son Ephraim. I always said so to him. And so it came to pass. He is my only son. His violin playing is extraordinary. You should ask him to play for you one day. But he is proud. Who knows if he will!' It was as though it was for me to thank the coachman Manes for giving me the opportunity to procure his son a place in the conservatory. 'I have no more business in Vienna,' so he continued, 'I am going home tomorrow.'

'You must call on Count Chojnicki, and thank him,' I told him.

'A fine Count!' said Manes, appreciatively. 'I will bid him adieu. Has he heard my Ephraim play?'

'No,' I said, 'you should ask him.'

The train of the coachman Manes Reisiger was leaving at eleven at night. At eight he came to me, asking, if not ordering, me to take him to Chojnicki's hotel.

Very well, I took him there. Chojnicki was grateful, almost delighted. Yes, he was even moved. 'How wonderful that he should come to me and thank me,' he said. 'I told you right away this is what our Jews are like!'

By the end, he was thanking the coachman Manes for giving him the opportunity of having preserved a genius for the world. It sounded as though for the last decade or more, Chojnicki had been waiting for nothing more than that the son of Manes Reisiger should come to him, and that now a long held and deeply desired wish was finally being fulfilled. In his gratitude, he even offered Manes Reisiger the fare for his return journey. This the coachman Manes declined, but he invited us both to visit him. He had a house, he told us, with three rooms and a kitchen, a stable for his horse, and a garden where he parked his carriage and his sleigh. He wasn't a poor coachman by any manner of means. He earned as much as fifty crowns a month. And if we visited him, we would have a wonderful time. He would certainly see to it that we lacked for nothing.

Nor did he forget to remind Chojnicki and me that it was positively our duty to look after his son Ephraim. 'A genius like that must be looked after!' he said, in leaving. Chojnicki promised to do just that; and also that we would visit him in Zlotogrod next summer, without fail.

# VII

At this point, it behoves me to speak of an important matter that I had hoped, as I began writing this book, to avoid. What is at issue is religion.

Like my friends, like all my friends, I had no faith. I never attended Mass. I would accompany my mother as far as the church door, my mother who herself may not have had faith, but who was, as people say, 'practicing'. At that time I had a positive hatred of the church. Today, now that I am a believer, I no longer know why I hated it so. It was, so to speak, the 'fashion'.

I would have felt ashamed to tell my friends that I had been to church. They were not really opposed to religion as such; it was more that there was a type of arrogance in them towards the tradition in which they had grown up. They didn't want to renounce the essence of the tradition, but they – and since I went along with them, we – rebelled against the forms, because we didn't know that true form is inseparable from essence, and that it was childish to try to separate them. It was childish, but as I say, we were children in those days. Death was already crossing his bony hands over the bumpers from which we drank in our childish merriment. We were unaware of him. We were unaware of him because we were unaware of God. Of our number, it was only Count Chojnicki who still observed the forms of religion, not so much from faith, as from a sort of *noblesse oblige*. The rest of us who disdained them were little better than anarchists in his view. 'The church of Rome,' so he would harangue us, 'is the only brace in this rotten world. The only giver and maintainer of form. By enshrining the traditional element "handed down" in its dogmas, as in an icy palace, it obtains and bestows upon its children the licence to play round about this icy palace, which has spacious grounds, to indulge irresponsibility, even to pardon the forbidden, or to enact it. By instituting sin, it forgives sins. It sees that there is no man without flaw: that is the wonderfully humane thing about it. Its flawless children become saints. By that alone, it concedes the flawed nature of mankind. It concedes sinfulness to such a degree even that it refuses to see beings as human if they are not sinful: they will be sainted or holy. In so doing the Church of Rome shows its most exalted tendency, namely to forgive. There is no nobler tendency than forgiveness. And by the same token, there is none more vulgar than to seek revenge. There is no nobility without generosity, just as there is no vengefulness without vulgarity.'

Count Chojnicki was the oldest and wisest of us, but we

were too young and foolish to give his superiority the attention it merited. We listened to him, complaisantly, and even imagined we were doing him a favour. To us, so-called young people, he was an elderly gentleman. Only later, in the War, did we come to see how much younger he truly was than we were.

It was only afterwards, and far too late, that we grasped that we were not younger than him, but quite simply ageless: unnatural, if you will, without age. While he, of course, in keeping with his years, was authentic and blessed.

# VIII

A few months later, I received the following letter from the coachman Manes Reisiger:

Dear Sir,

After the great honour and service you did me, I humbly permit myself to inform you that I am very, very grateful to you. My son writes to tell me he is doing well at the conservatory, and I owe you thanks for his genius. I thank you from the bottom of my heart. At the same time, I humbly permit myself to ask you to do me the great kindness of paying me a visit. Your cousin, the chestnut roaster Trotta, always – which is to say, for the past ten years – stays with me in the autumn. I imagine that you too might find pleasure in staying with me. My house is poor, but spacious.

Esteemed sir! Don't despise this invitation. I am so

small, and you are so great. Dear sir! I also beg your forgiveness for having this letter written. I cannot write, except my own name. The present letter is written on my instructions by the official public scribe of our town, Hirsch Kiniower, who is a dependable, tidy, and officially licensed individual. Signed, your obedient servant:

Manes Reisiger, Coachman, Zlotogrod

The whole letter was written in a careful, calligraphic hand, of the sort that was then described as 'like a book'. Only the writing of the name, the signature, betrayed the enchanting clumsiness of the coachman's hand. That signature alone would have been sufficient to decide me to keep my word, and travel to Zlotogrod in early autumn. All of us in those days were carefree, and I was as carefree as any of the others. Our life before the Great War was idyllic, and a journey to the faraway town of Zlotogrod seemed like an adventure to all of us.

And the fact that I was to be the hero of this adventure was a splendid opportunity to strike a pose before my friends. And even though this adventurous journey was so far in the future, and even though I was going alone, we talked about it every evening, as though there was only a week between me and Zlotogrod, and as though it wasn't just me alone, but all of us who were going. Gradually the journey became a passion for us, an obsession even. And we started to paint an imaginary picture of the remote little town of Zlotogrod, to such a degree that even while we were describing it, we were convinced we were painting wholly inaccurate pictures; and we couldn't stop distorting this place none of us had ever seen. I mean: giving it all sorts of attributes of which we were sure in advance that they were products of our imagination, and not at all the real properties of the little town.

Untroubled times! Death was already crossing his bony hands over the glass bumpers from which we drank. We didn't see him; we didn't even see his hands. We talked so long and so intently about Zlotogrod that I began to be afraid it might suddenly disappear, or that my friends might come to the conclusion that it was all talk, and that such a Zlotogrod didn't in fact exist and that it was a figment of my imagination. Suddenly I was seized with an impatient longing for Zlotogrod, and for the coachman by the name of Reisiger.

In the middle of the summer of 1914 I went there, having first written to my cousin Trotta in Sipolje that I hoped to meet him there.

# IX

So, in the middle of the summer of 1914, I went to Zloto-grod. I put up at the Golden Bear, the only hotel in the little town, so I was told, that was up to European standards.

The station was tiny, just like the station in Sipolje, which I had dutifully committed to memory. All the stations in the old Dual Monarchy resembled each other, all the little stations in the little provincial towns. Yellow and tiny, they were like lazy cats that in winter lay in the snow, in summer in the sun, sheltering under the crystal glass roofs over the platform, and guarded by the emblem of the black double eagle on yellow ground. All over, in Sipolje as in Zlotogrod, there was the same porter, the same porter with the impressive belly, the peaceable dark blue uniform, the black sash diagonally across the chest, the sash in which the bell was stuck, the bell from which issued the three-fold official ring that was the signal for departure; on the platform in Zlotogrod, over the door to the stationmaster's office, as in Sipolje and everywhere else, hung that black iron instrument that so miraculously produced the distant silver tinkle of the distant telephone, douce and frail signals from other worlds, so that one was surprised that they had found a home in such a heavy, albeit small earpiece; on the station in Zlotogrod, as on the station in Sipolje, the porter saluted the arrivals and the departures, and his saluting conferred a sort of military benediction; in the station in Zlotogrod, as in the station in Sipolje, there was the same 'first and second class waiting room', the same station buffet, with the row of schnapps bottles and the bosomy·blonde cashier and the two gigantic potted palms either side of the bar, that were equally reminiscent of primitive vegetation and cardboard beer-mats. And outside the station, exactly as in Sipolje, stood three coaches. And I straight-away recognized the unmistakeable coachman, Manes Reisiger.

Of course, it was he who took me to the Golden Bear. He had a fine carriage drawn by a pair of silvery greys, the spokes of the wheels were painted yellow, and the tyres were rubber, just as Manes had seen them in Vienna, on the so-called 'rubber-wheelers'.

He admitted to me as we drove that he had reconditioned his coach, not so much for my comfort and in my honour, as out of a sort of collective zeal that compelled him to take a leaf out of the book of his colleagues, the Viennese coachmen, and sac-rifice his savings to the god of progress, and invest in two greys, and put rubber tyres on his wheels.

From the station to the town was a substantial distance, and Manes Reisiger had plenty of time to tell me the things that were on his mind. As he did so, he held the reins in his left hand. On his right, the whip stayed in its case. The greys needed no instruction, seeming to know the way. Manes didn't need to do anything. So he sat there casually on the box, with the reins in a loose grip in his left hand, half-turned towards me while he talked. The two greys had cost just one hundred and twenty-five crowns. They were army horses, both blind in one eye, and so no longer useful for military purposes, and sold cheap by the Ninth Dragoons, who were stationed in Zlotogrod. Admittedly he, the coachman Manes Reisiger, would never have been able to buy them so easily, if he hadn't happened to be a favourite of the Colonel of the Ninth Dragoons. In the little town of Zlotogrod there were no fewer than five coachmen. The other four, Reisiger's colleagues, had dirty cabs, lazy, hobbling old mares, crooked wheels, and scabbed leather benches. The stuffing swelled up out of the patched and holey leather, and no gentleman, much less a Colonel of the Ninth Dragoons, could be expected to sit in such a coach.

I had letters from Chojnicki to the commanding officer of the local garrison, Colonel Földes of the Ninth, and also to the District Commissioner, Baron Grappik. The following morning, on the first full day of my stay, I proposed to pay calls on both men. The coachman Manes Reisiger fell silent, he had nothing more to say, having already told me everything important in his life. Even so, he left the whip in its case, still held the reins nice and loose, still sat half-turned towards me on the box. The steady smile on his wide mouth, with the strong white teeth against the night-black, almost blue-black blackness of his beard and moustaches suggested a milky moon between forests, between agreeable forests. There was so much cheer, so much goodness in that smile, that it even contrived to dominate the flat, melancholy landscape I was driving through. Wide fields on my right, and wide swamps on my left bordered the road between the Zlotogrod railway station and the little town of Zlotogrod itself – it was as though it had taken some vow of chastity and sworn to keep away from the station that connected it to the world at large. It was a rainy afternoon, and, as I say, early autumn. The rubber tyres of Manes's carriage rolled soundlessly along the sodden, unpaved road, while the heavy hooves of the ex-Army greys smacked rhythmically into the dark grey mud, sending great clumps of it flying through the air. Darkness was falling when we reached the first houses. In the middle of the Ring, facing the little church, its presence marked by a solitary sorry lantern, stood Zlotogrod's one and only two-storey building: it was the Golden Bear. The solitary lantern was like an orphan child, vainly trying to smile through its tears.

Even with so much that was unfamiliar, or more, that was remote and distant for which I had prepared myself, most of what I saw was homely and familiar. It wasn't till much later – long after the Great War, which people call the 'World War', and in my view rightly, and not for the usual reason, that the whole world was involved in it, but rather because as a result of it we lost a whole world, our world – not till much later, then, was it that I would see that even landscapes, fields, nations, races, huts and cafés of all sorts and origins must follow the natural law of a strong spirit that is capable of bringing the far near, making the exotic familiar, and bringing together things that are pulling apart. I am referring to the misunderstood and maligned spirit of the old Monarchy, which allowed me to feel every bit as much at home in Zlotogrod as I did in Sipolje, or in Vienna for that matter. The only café in Zlotogrod, the Café Habsburg, situated on the ground floor of the hotel where I was staying, the Golden Bear, looked not a whit different from the Café Wimmerl in Josefstadt, where I was in the habit of meeting my friends in the afternoons. Here too behind the bar sat the familiar figure of the cashier, a voluptuous blonde of a type that seemed to be the exclusive preserve of cashiers in my time, a stolid goddess of vice, a seductress so obvious – lustful, destructive and professionally patient – that she contented herself with mere hints. I had seen her like in Agram, in Olmütz, in Brünn, in Kecskemet, in Szombathely, in Ödenburg, in Sternberg, in Müglitz. The chessboards and dominoes, the smoke-stained walls, the gaslights, the kitchen table in the corner by the door to the toilets, the maid in her blue apron, the local constable with his clay-coloured helmet stepping in for a break, equally sheepish and intimidating, leaving his rifle with fixed bayonet almost shyly in the umbrella holder, and the tarock players with their Franz Joseph mutton-chops and their round cuffs, foregathering every day at the same time – all this was home and it was more than country or fatherland, it was a wide and varied expanse, but it was still familiar and homely: it was the Dual Monarchy of Austria-Hungary. District Commissioner Baron Grappik and Colonel Földes of the Ninth both spoke the same nasal army German of the better classes, a language that was harsh and soft at the same time, as though it had been sired by Slavs and Italians, a language full of discreet irony and ornate assurances of beholdenness, and of gossip, and even of mild nonsense. Before a week was out, I felt as much at home in Zlotogrod as I had in Sipolje, or Müglitz, or Brünn, or in our Café Wimmerl in the Josefstadt.

Of course I went for rides every day in the cab of my friend Manes Reisiger. The country was in actual fact poor, but it looked blithe and flush. Even the expanse of swamp where nothing grew looked juicy and bountiful to me, and the good-natured chorus of frogs that emanated from it was a hymn of praise from creatures who happened to have an acuter understanding than I did of the purpose for which the Almighty had created their home, the swamps.

At night I sometimes heard the hoarse, broken cries of the wild geese flying high above. There was still plenty of green on the willows and birches, but the magnificent chestnuts were already shedding their tough, bronze, precisely silhouetted leaves. The ducks chattered in the middle of the road, where the silver-grey mud, never completely dry, was punctuated by occasional ponds.

I usually ate my dinner with the officers of the Ninth Dragoons; or, more accurately, drank it. Over the glass bumpers from which we drank, an invisible Death was already crossing his bony hands. We didn't sense them. Sometimes we sat together till late. Out of an inexplicable fear of the night, we stayed up till dawn.

An inexplicable fear, I say, though to us at the time it seemed rational; we sought an explanation in the claim that we were too young to neglect the nights. In fact, as I saw later, it was our fear of the day, more precisely, our fear of morning, the clearest portion of the day. That's when a man can see and is himself seen with the greatest clarity. And we had no desire either to see, or to be seen clearly.

In the morning, then, to escape that clarity, and also the dull, unrefreshing sleep that I knew all too well, and that overcomes a man after a night on the tiles like a false friend, a quack doctor, a sullen well-wisher, or a treacherous benefactor, I took refuge with Manes, the coachman. I often turned up around six in the morning, just as he was getting up. He lived outside the town, close to the cemetery. It took me half an hour to get there on foot. I would arrive sometimes just as he had got out of bed. His little house stood there all by itself, surrounded by fields and meadows that didn't belong to him, painted blue, and with a grey black shingled roof, not unlike a living creature that seemed not to stand, but to be in motion So strong was the deep blue of the walls against the slowly waning yellow-green that surrounded it on all sides. When I pushed open the red gate that barred the way to the coachman Manes's residence, I sometimes caught him standing in his doorway. He would be standing in front of the brown door, in his homespun shirt and drawers, barefoot and bare-headed, holding a large brown can in his hand. He would take a sup from it, then spit out the water in a great arc. With his great black beard, staring into the rising sun, in his coarse linens, with his wild and woolly hair, he was redolent of jungle, primitive, primordial, confused and misplaced, who knew why.

He pulled off his shirt and washed himself at the well. He spluttered and snorted as he did so, spat, howled and roared, it really was like the primitive invading our time. Then he pulled on his coarse shirt, and we each advanced to exchange greetings. Our greetings were in equal part formal and heartfelt. There was a kind of ceremony about them, though we saw each other almost every morning, a tacit assurance that to me he was more than a Jewish coachman, while for him I was more than a young whippersnapper from the capital, with influential friends. Sometimes he asked me to read the rare letters his son wrote him from the conservatory. They were short letters, but since in the first place he didn't have a very good grasp of the German in which his son felt obliged to write – goodness only knows why – and secondly because his tender father's heart wanted these letters to be a little less short than they were, he made sure I read them to him very slowly. Often he would ask me to repeat a sentence two or three times.

The chickens in his little shed started to cluck as soon as he set foot in the yard. The horses whinnied, almost lustfully, to the morning and to Manes the coachman. First, he unlocked the stable, and both greys put out their heads at once. He kissed them both, as a man kisses a woman. Then he went into the shed to get out the carriage. Thereupon, he put the horses to. Then he opened the henhouse, and with much squawking and flapping of wings the fowls scattered. It was as though an invisible hand had dispersed them across the yard.

I also saw the wife of the coachman Manes Reisiger. She got

up about half an hour after her husband, and asked me in to tea. I drank it, from the great tin samovar in their blue kitchen, while Manes ate his bread and onion with grated radish and cucumbers. It smelled strong, but secret, almost homely. I had never breakfasted in this way before, but I loved it, I was young, really I was just young.

I even liked the wife of my friend Manes Reisiger, though she was what in common parlance is called plain, red-haired, freckled, looking like a puffed-up bread roll. In spite of that, and in spite of her fat fingers, there was something dainty about the way she poured my tea and prepared her husband's breakfast. She had given him three children. Two had died of smallpox. She would talk about the dead children sometimes, as though they were still alive. She seemed not to distinguish between those of her children who were in the ground and her son who had gone off to the conservatory in Vienna; perhaps to her he was as good as dead. Certainly, he was no longer present in her life.

Someone who was eminently alive to her and always present in her imagination was my cousin, the chestnut roaster. I drew my own conclusions. In another week he would be with us, my cousin Joseph Branco Trotta.

# X

And in another week, he arrived.

He arrived with his mule, his leather sack and his chestnuts. He was dark and tan and jovial, just as he was when I had last seen him in Vienna. It felt perfectly normal to him to see me here. The proper chestnut season was still a while off. My cousin had simply come a couple of weeks early on my account. On the way from the station into town, he sat on the box alongside our mutual friend, the coachman Manes Reisiger. He had tethered his mule to the cab. His leather sack, his pan and his chestnuts were strapped to either side. And so we made our entry into the little town of Zlotogrod, but we aroused no interest. The people of Zlotogrod were used to seeing my cousin Joseph Branco turning up every other year. And they seemed to have already got used to me, the stranger in their midst.

As usual, my cousin Joseph Branco stayed with Manes Reisiger. Mindful of the deals he had struck with me the

previous summer for his watch and chain, he had packed a few
more knick-knacks for me, for instance an embossed silver ashtray with two crossed daggers and a St Nicodemus (who had
nothing to do with them), also a brass mug that seemed to me
to smell of sour dough, and a painted wooden cuckoo. All
these, thus Joseph Branco, were presents for me, 'in consideration of' his travel expenses. And I understood what he meant
by 'in consideration of'. I bought the ashtray, the mug and the
wooden bird from him on the evening of his arrival. He was
happy.

To while away the time, as he claimed, but in fact to take
every opportunity of earning a little money, he made occasional
attempts to persuade the coachman Manes that he, Joseph
Branco, was a skilled coachman, better than Manes, and better
able too to find customers. But Reisiger paid no attention.
Without bothering about Joseph Branco, he put his horses to
early in the morning, and drove off to the station and to the
market place, where his colleagues, the other coachmen waited.

It was a fine, sunny summer. Even though Zlotogrod wasn't
a proper 'little town' at all, being rather more of a village in disguise; and even though it gave off the fresh breath of nature, to
such an extent that the forests, swamps and hills that surrounded
it almost seemed to cluster round the marketplace, and you got
the impression that forest, swamp and hill might just as easily
and naturally march into town as any traveller arriving at the
station to put up at the Golden Bear; my friends, the officials in
the District Commissioner's office, and the gentlemen of the
Ninth Dragoons were of the view that Zlotogrod was a real

town, because they needed to think they hadn't been banished to the end of the earth, and the mere fact that there was a railway station in Zlotogrod gave them the assurance that they didn't live remote from the civilisation they had grown up in and that had pampered them. The result was that once or twice a week they claimed to have to leave the unbreathable town air, pile into carriages, and head for the forests, swamps and hills that in actual fact were on their way into town to them. Because not only was Zlotogrod full of nature, it also seemed to be under siege from its surroundings. So it happened that once or twice a week I and my friends went out in Manes Reisiger's cab into the so-called 'environs' of Zlotogrod. We referred to these trips as 'outings'. Often we would stop at Jadlowker's frontier tavern. Old Jadlowker, an ancient, silver-bearded Jew, sat outside the mighty arch of his broad, grass-green double-doors, stiff and half-paralysed. He resembled winter who wanted to enjoy the last fine days of autumn and take them with him into the rapidly approaching eternity that would know no more seasons. He couldn't hear, not one word, he was deaf as a post. But from his large, sad, black eyes I thought I could tell that everything that younger men took in with their ears, he was able to see, and that his deafness was a chosen deafness that he was happy in. The threads of gossamer flew gently and tenderly past him. The silvery, but still warm autumn sun shone on the old man as he sat facing west, facing the evening and the sunset, the terrestrial emblems of death, as though he expected that the eternity to which he would soon be consigned would come to him, rather than he go out to it. The crickets shrilled incessantly. The frogs croaked incessantly. A deep peace ruled over the world, the bitter peace of autumn.

At about this time, my cousin Joseph Branco, following an old-established tradition among the chestnut roasters of Austria-Hungary, would open his stall on the Ring of Zlotogrod. For two days the warm, chewy smell of baked apples wafted through the little town.

It began to rain. It was a Thursday. The following day, a Friday therefore, the news was on all street-corners.

It was a proclamation from our old Emperor Franz Joseph, and it was addressed: 'To my peoples'.

# XI

I was an ensign in the Reserve. It was only two years previously that I had left my battalion, the Twenty-First Jägers. At the time it seemed to me that the war had come at a good moment. Now that it was there and inevitable, I saw right away – and it seems to me my friends will have seen it just as spontaneously – that even a meaningless death was better than a meaningless life. I was afraid of death. No question. I didn't want to die. All I wanted was the certainty that I would know how to die.

My friend Joseph Branco and his friend the cabbie Manes were both reservists. They were drafted. On the evening of the Friday when the Emperor's proclamation was put up on walls everywhere, I went, as usual, to the officers' mess, to eat with my friends in the Ninth Dragoons. I couldn't understand their healthy appetite, their standard good cheer, their foolish equanimity in view of their orders to attack the Russian frontier town of Radziwillow to the northeast. I was the only one among them who saw the signs of death in their harmless, even cheerful, certainly unmoved expressions. It was as though they were in that state of euphoria that is sometimes experienced by people near death, and that is itself an avatar of death. And even though they were healthy and alert as they sat at their tables drinking their schnapps and their beer, and even though I pretended to take part in their tomfooleries and japes, yet I felt more like a doctor or medical orderly who sees his patient dying, thankful only that the dying man seems unaware of his imminent death. And yet in the long run I still felt unease of a kind that the doctor or orderly may feel when confronted with death and the dying man's euphoria, at that instant when they are not quite sure whether it might not be better to tell the doomed man what awaits him, instead of feeling relief that he might depart without guessing.

As a result I quickly left the gentlemen of the Ninth Dragoons, and set off on my way to Manes the cabbie, with whom, as already said, my cousin Joseph Branco was staying.

How different was the feeling there, and how salutary it was for me after that evening in the mess of the Ninth Dragoons! Maybe it was the ritual candles in the blue parlour of the Jewish cabbie Manes, burning almost cheerfully, but in any case stolidly and fearlessly, towards their extinction; three candles, golden yellow, stuck in green beer bottles; the cabbie Manes was too poor even to buy himself brass candlesticks. They were little more than stumps of candles, and they seemed to me to symbolize the end of the world, which I knew was now at hand. The tablecloth was white, the bottles of that cheap green glass that seems to proclaim its refreshing contents in a plebeian and exuberant manner, and the flickering candle ends were golden yellow. They were guttering. They cast a restless light over the table, and projected equally restless, flickering shadows on the dark blue walls. At the head of the table sat Manes the cabbie, not in his usual cabbie's gear of belted sheepskin and corduroy cap, but in a shiny three-quarter-length coat and a black velvet cap. My cousin Joseph Branco wore the greasy leather jerkin he always wore, and, out of respect for his Jewish host, a green Tyrolean hat on his head. Somewhere a cricket was chirruping shrilly.

'The time has come for us all to say our goodbyes,' began Manes the cabbie. And, much more clear-sighted than my friends in the Ninth Dragoons, and yet with an almost aristo-cratic touch of equanimity, because of the way death exalts every man who is both prepared for it and worthy of it, he con-tinued: 'It will be a great war, a long war, and there is no knowing which of us may one day come home from it. For the last time I am sitting here, at the side of my wife, at the Friday table, with the Sabbath candles. Let us take a proper farewell, my friends: you, Branco, and you, sir!' And, in order to take a truly proper farewell, we decided, the three of us, to go to Jadlowker's border tavern.

# XII

Jadlowker's border tavern was always open, at all times of day and night. It was the bar for Russian deserters, those of the Tsar's soldiers, that is, who could be persuaded, cajoled or threatened by the numerous agents of the American shipping lines to leave the army, and take ship for Canada. Many more, admittedly, quit voluntarily. They paid the agents the last money they had; they or their relations. Jadlowker's border tavern had the reputation of a disorderly house. But, like all the other disorderly houses in the area, it was commended to the favour of the Austrian border police, and thus in a manner of speaking enjoyed simultaneously the protection and the suspicion of the authorities.

When we got there – at the end of a silent and depressed half-hour walk – the great, brown double-doors were already locked. Even the lantern that hung there was out. We were forced to knock, and the boy Onufri came to let us in. I knew

Jadlowker's tavern, I had been there a couple of times, and I was familiar with the usual commotion of the place, that particular type of noise that is made by people who have suddenly become homeless or stateless, who have no present, because they are transiting from the past into the future, from a familiar past to a highly doubtful future, like ship's passengers at the moment that they leave terra firma to board an unfamiliar ship by way of a wobbling gangplank.

Today, though, was quiet. It was eerily quiet. Even little Kapturak, one of the keenest and noisiest agents, whose preferred way of hiding all the many things he was professionally and personally obliged to hide was by means of an extreme garrulousness, today sat silently in the corner, on the bench by the stove, small, tinier than he was already, and thus doubly inconspicuous, a silent shadow of his otherwise self. Only the day before yesterday he had escorted a group of deserters, or as they like to say in his calling, a 'consignment', over the frontier, and now the Emperor's proclamation was on every wall, the war was there, even the mighty shipping agency was powerless, the mighty thunder of world history silenced the chattersome little Kapturak, and its violent lightning reduced him to a shadow. The deserters, Kapturak's victims, sat with dull and glazed expressions in front of their half-filled glasses. Each time I'd gone to Jadlowker's tavern before, it had been a particular pleasure of mine — as a young, glib person, who sees in the foolish behaviour of others, even the most exotic and alien, due confirmation of his own thoughtlessness — to spectate at the insouciance of those recently become stateless, the way they drained one glass after another, and ordered one glass after another. The landlord Jadlowker sat behind his bar like an omen, not a messenger of doom, but its bearer; he looked as though he didn't have the least inclination to fill any glasses, even if his customers had called for it. What was the point of it all? Tomorrow or the day after, the Russians might be here. Poor Jadlowker, who even a week ago had sat there so majestically with his silver beard, like a lord mayor among the barmen, shadowed and protected as much by the discreet protection of the authorities as by their creditable mistrust, today looked like a human being who is obliged to liquidize his entire existence: a victim of world history. And the heavy blonde barmaid at his side behind the bar had also just been terminated by world history, and given in her brief notice. Everything private was suddenly out in the open. It represented the public world, it stood in for and symbolized it. That was why our farewells were so misguided and so brief. We drank three glasses of mead, and with them we silently munched salted peas. Suddenly my cousin Joseph Branco said: 'I'm not going back to Sarajevo. I'm going to report here in Zloczow, together with Manes!' 'Bravo!' I exclaimed. And as I did, I knew I would have liked to do exactly the same thing.

But I was thinking about Elisabeth.

# XIII

I was thinking about Elisabeth. Ever since I had read the Emperor's proclamation, I had only two thoughts in my head: one was of death, and the other was of Elisabeth. To this day I don't know which of them was stronger.

Faced with death, all my foolish anxieties about the foolish jeers of my friends vanished and were forgotten. All at once, I felt brave, for the first time in my life I had courage to own up to my so-called 'weakness'. I sensed that the facile exuberance of my friends in Vienna would have recoiled before the black gleam of death, and that in the hour of farewell – of such a farewell – there could be no space for any sort of mockery.

I too could have reported for duty to the local recruiting office in Zloczow, where the cabbie Manes was expected and where my cousin Joseph Branco was also going. In fact, it was my intention to forget Elisabeth and my friends in Vienna and my mother, and deliver myself as soon as possible to the nearest receiving station of death, which is to say, the local recruiting office in Zloczow. Strong feelings bound me to my cousin Joseph Branco and his friend the cabbie Manes Reisiger. Given the nearness of death, my feelings became purer and clearer, just as sometimes, with the onset of a grave illness, clear insights and priorities emerge, so that, for all one's apprehension and anxiety and sense of suffering to come, a sort of proud satisfaction sets in that one has understood something; the happiness one has identified in suffering, and a sort of serenity because one has been presented with the bill in advance. We are almost happy in our illness. I was just as happy in contemplation of the great illness that was breaking out in the world, which is to say the World War. I could allow my fever dreams their course, which otherwise I tried to suppress. I was in equal measure liberated and endangered.

I already knew that my cousin Joseph Branco and his friend Manes Reisiger were dearer to me than all my erstwhile friends, with the exception of Count Chojnicki. People's notions of the war ahead were simplistic and for the most part ridiculous. I myself supposed we would march by garrisons, probably in closed ranks, and if not side by side, then at least remain in hailing distance. I pictured myself as I wished to be: in close proximity to my cousin Joseph Branco and his friend, the cabbie Manes.

But there was no time to lose. In fact, what chiefly oppressed us in those days was haste: there was no more time to fill the negligible amount of space left us by our lives, not even time to ready ourselves to die. We didn't really know whether to yearn for death or hope to escape with our lives. For me and the likes of me these were hours of utmost tension: hours in which death no longer looked like an abyss that you plunge into one day, more like a further shore that you try to leap across to, and you know how long the seconds feel before you leap.

I went first to my mother's, as though following some prompting of nature. It was clear that she didn't think she would see me again, but she pretended to be expecting me. It's one of the secrets of mothers: they never pass up a chance to see their offspring, whether supposed dead or actually dead; and if it were possible for a dead son to be resurrected, she would take him in her arms as promptly as though he hadn't returned from the hereafter, but merely from the reaches of here somewhere. A mother is always expecting the return of her son: whether he's near or far or dead. It was in such a spirit that my mother welcomed me at nine o'clock that morning. She was sitting there as ever, in her chair, having just finished her breakfast, with the newspaper in front of her and her old-fashioned oval steel-rimmed spectacles on. She took them off when I walked in, but she didn't lower her newspaper. 'I kiss your hand, Mother!' I said, walked up to her, and took the newspaper from her. I fell into her lap. She kissed me on the mouth, the cheeks, the brow. 'So it's war,' she said, as though she was breaking the news to me, or as though the war had only begun with the moment of my return home to say goodbye.

'Yes,' I replied, 'it's war, and I've come to say goodbye to you.' 'And also,' I added after a while, 'to marry Elisabeth before I join up.'

'Why marry,' asked my mother, 'if you're off to the war?' Here too, she was speaking like a mother. If she was letting her son – her only son – go off to the war, then she wanted to be sure she was delivering him into the hands of death, and death alone. She didn't want to share her possession or her loss with another woman.

She had probably guessed for a long time that I was in love with Elisabeth. (She knew her.) My mother had probably been afraid for a long time that she would lose her only son to another woman – which seemed on balance worse than losing him to death. 'Son of mine,' she said, 'you are old enough to decide what you want to do with your life. You want to get married before you go to war; I understand. I am not a man, I have never experienced war, I know little of the army. But I know that war is something terrible, and that you may very well die in the course of it. At this time I can be blunt with you. I don't care for Elisabeth. I would never have stood in the way of your marrying her, not even under normal circumstances. But I wouldn't have been blunt with you. Marry her and be happy, if circumstances permit. And there's an end. Now, let's talk about other things: when are you reporting? And where?'

For the first time in my life I felt sheepish, even a little insignificant, in front of my mother. I had no other answer to give than a rather pathetic: 'I'm sure I'll be back soon, Mama!' which still sounds wretched in my ears today.

'Be back by lunchtime, son,' she said, the way she always did, and as though the world were perfectly in order, 'we're having schnitzel and plum dumplings for lunch.'

It was a classic display of motherhood: my readiness to die suddenly trumped by the peaceful dumplings. I could have fallen to my knees with emotion. But I was still too young at the time to be able to show emotion without embarrassment. I've since learned that it takes great maturity and experience for a man to display emotion without embarrassment.

I kissed my mother's hand, as I always did. Her hand – how could I ever forget it – was slender and delicate and veined with blue. The morning light swept into the room, a little dimmed by the dark red silk curtains, like a well-behaved guest dressed in formal attire. The pale hand of my mother took on a reddish shimmer as well, a kind of blushing scarlet, a hallowed hand gloved in morning sunlight. And the hesitant autumnal twitter of the birds in our garden was almost as familiar and almost as remote to me as the familiar red-veiled hand of my mother.

'I have to go,' was all I said. I went to see the father of my dearly loved Elisabeth.

# XIV

The father of my dearly loved Elisabeth was at that time a prominent, almost a celebrated, hat-maker. He had gone from a ten-a-penny 'imperial councillor' to a common-or-garden Hungarian baron The positively arcane customs of the old Monarchy sometimes called for Austrian commercial councillors to become Hungarian barons.

The war came at a not unwelcome juncture for my future father-in-law. He was already too old to have to serve, but still young enough to make the leap from a respectable solid hat-maker to a dashing manufacturer of those army caps that bring in so much more profit and cost so much less to produce than a topper.

It was noon, the bells in the Rathaus were just striking, and when I walked in, he was just back from a highly satisfactory meeting at the War Ministry. He had been given a contract to make half a million army caps. In this way, he told me, an ageing helpless man could still serve his fatherland. As he spoke, he kept running his hands through his greying blond whiskers, as though to caress both halves of the Dual Monarchy, its Cis- and Transleithanian wings. He was big, heavy and slow. He made me think of a sort of sunny porter who had undertaken to make half a million caps, and whom such a burden, far from weighing him down, made lighter. 'Well, I suppose you'll be reporting for duty then!' he said in positively genial tones. 'I don't think I'm giving anything away if I say my daughter will miss you.'

At that moment, I saw I couldn't possibly ask him for his daughter's hand in marriage. And with that impetuosity with which one tries to make the impossible possible, and that haste with which an ever-advancing death compelled me to seize whatever remained of my life, I was brusque with the hat-maker: 'I need to speak to your daughter right away.'

'My young friend,' he replied, 'I know you want to ask for her hand in marriage. I know Elisabeth won't turn you down. So why don't you just take mine for the moment, and see yourself as my son!' And with that he put out his large, soft and far too white hand. I took it and had the sensation of paddling around in some hopeless pastry dough. It was a hand without pressure and without warmth. It gave the lie to his offer of making me his 'son', it even rescinded it. Elisabeth came in, and the hat-maker saved me the trouble of speaking. 'Herr Trotta is away to the war' – thus my father-in-law, as if to say I was going to the Riviera for a holiday – 'but he would like to marry you first.'

He spoke in the same tones he had used an hour before in the War Ministry, talking to the equipment johnnies about forage caps. But there was Elisabeth. There was her smile, seeming to float ahead of her towards me, a light that was born in her, and seemed everlasting and eternally renewable, a silvery bliss that seemed to tinkle, though it was silent.

We fell into each other's arms. We kissed for the very first time, passionately, shamelessly almost, in spite of her father's presence, yes, perhaps even with the blissful criminal awareness of having a witness to our indiscretion. I told her the situation. I had no time. Death stood at my back. I was its son, more than I was the son of any hat-maker. I had to join my Twenty-First, on the Landstrasser Hauptstrasse. I hurried off, straight from Elisabeth's embrace into the army; from love to destruction. I relished them both with the same fortitude of heart. I hailed a cab, and trundled off to the barracks.

I met friends and comrades there. Some of them, like me, were coming straight out of embraces.

# XV

They came straight out of embraces, and they had the sense that they had already performed the critical part of their warriors' duties. They had set a date for their weddings. Each of them had lined up some girl or other to marry, even if it wasn't a proper match but a chance hook-up of a kind that in those times for unknown reasons seemed to come fluttering along from who knew where, not unlike moths fluttering in through an open window on a summer night to our tables and beds and mantelpieces – fluttering, flighty, effortless, devoted, the velvety gifts of a brief and generous night. If peace had continued, each of us would surely have held out against a legal marriage. It was only heirs to the throne who were required to marry. At thirty, our fathers were all dignified paterfamiliases and heads of households. But in us, foredoomed to war from birth, the reproductive urge had manifestly faded. We had no very great desire to procreate. Death crossed its bony hands not only above the glass bumpers from which we drank, but also over the beds in which at night we slept with our women. And that was perhaps why there was something so lackadaisical about our women in those days. We didn't even greatly care for the pleasure of sex.

But now, now that war suddenly summoned us to the reserve depots, it wasn't the thought of death that it bred in us, but that of honour, and its sister, danger. Honour is an anaesthetic, and what it anaesthetized in us was fear and foreboding. When a man is on his deathbed, and draws up his will and settles his worldly accounts, he will experience a certain tremor. But we were young and healthy! We could feel no tremor, not really; it just suited us, flattered us to evoke the idea of it in our relatives. Yes, we made our wills out of vanity; out of vanity we married in haste, with a headlong rush that precluded thought or even remorse. Marriage made us appear nobler than we already were by virtue of our sacrifice. For us it made death (which we feared but still preferred to a lifelong commitment) less dangerous and less ugly. We burned our bridges. And that first unforgettable and fine elan with which we advanced into those first terrible battles was surely fuelled by our fear of retreating into 'settled domesticity', fear of gouty furniture, of wives who lost their attractiveness, of children who came into the world lovely as angels only to turn into hateful and monstrous strangers. No, we didn't want any of that. Danger was unavoidable. But to sweeten it, we got engaged. And so we went out to meet it, like an unknown but already beckoning and half-familiar home . . .

Even so, and although I knew I felt just like them, compared to my cousin Joseph Branco and his friend the Jewish cabbie Manes Reisiger, my comrades, as I record their names here, Reserve Ensign Bärenfels, Lieutenant Hartmann, First Lieutenant Linck, Baron Lerch and Officer Cadet Dr Brociner, struck me as superficial, frivolous, uncomradely, dull and unworthy both of the death they were going to meet, and of the settlements and weddings they were in the process of arranging. Of course I loved my Twenty-First Jägers! The old K-and-K army had a patriotism all of its own, a patriotism of regions, regiments and units. Militarily speaking, I had grown up with Sergeant Marek, with Corporal Türling, with Lance Corporal Alois Huber during my service and later on, during the annual manoeuvres. And of course one grows up a second time in the army: just as a child learns to walk, so a recruit learns to march. A man never forgets the recruits who learned to march at the same time as him, and to clean rifles and train with rifles, the packing of a haversack, and the regulation way to make a bed, to roll up a coat, to spit and polish boots, and night duty, Service Regulation part two, and the definitions: subordination and discipline, Service Regulation, part one. You never forget them or the water meadows you jogged around, with elbows tucked, and in late autumn the physical training, the grey mist turning every silver fir into a blue-grey widow, and the clearing in front of us, where soon, after the ten o'clock break, the field training would begin, the idyllic envoys of the real, scarlet war. You don't forget. The water meadows of the Twenty-First regiment were my home.

But my comrades were so cheerful about it all! We sat in the little bar that wasn't really a bar, not from the beginning, not from birth so to speak. Rather in the course of the many, almost innumerable years where our barracks, the barracks of the Twenty-First, had been situated and established here, it had evolved from an army outfitter's, where you could buy braid, pips, one-year-service badges, rosettes and bootlaces, into a bar. Gold braid was still stocked on the shelves. The dingy atmosphere was still more redolent of cardboard boxes of stars – the ones of white rubber, the ones of gold silk, and the rosettes for military officials, and the sword knots, which looked like concentrated showers of gold – than of apple juice, schnapps and old Gumpoldskirchner. In front of the counter, three or four little tables were set up. They were about as long-serving as we were. In fact, we had acquired them, and Zinker the owner had obtained his alcohol licence simply because our battalion commander, Major Pauli, had supported it. Civilians were not allowed to drink at Zinker's. The licence was for uniformed personnel only.

So there we were, huddled together again, in the outfitter's, just as once in our volunteer year. And the blitheness of my comrades, toasting our victory, just as years before they had drunk to our approaching officer's exams, deeply offended me. It's possible that my prophetic sense was just then unusually strong, my sense that while my comrades might manage to scrape through their officers' exams, given an actual war, they would fail. They had grown up in a pampered Vienna that was continually kept supplied by the Crown Lands of the Monarchy, naive, almost absurdly naive children of the celebrated and cossetted and over-mythologized Capital and Residence City, which sat, like a gleaming seductive spider, in the middle of a great black and yellow web, continually drawing strength and juice and glitter from the surrounding Crown Lands. The taxes that my poor cousin the chestnut roaster Joseph Branco Trotta paid in Sipolje, and the taxes that my impoverished Jewish cabbie Manes Reisiger paid in Zlotogrod went on maintaining the proud houses on the Ring belonging to the ennobled Jewish family Todesco, and the public buildings, the Parliament, the Law Courts, the University, the Land Credit Bank, the National Theatre, the Opera, and even the Police Presidium. The gaudy serenity of the Imperial Capital and Residence City was very clearly sustained – my father had often said so – by the tragic love of the Crown Lands for Austria, tragic because not recip-rocated. The gypsies from the Puszta, the sub-Carpathian Hutsuls, the Jewish cabbies from Galicia, my own relatives, the Slovene chestnut roasters from the Bačka, the horse-breeders from the steppe, the Ottoman Sibersna from Bosnia and Herzegovina, the horse-traders from the Haná in Moravia, the weavers from the Erzgebirge, the millers and coral sellers from Podolia: they were the great-hearted feeders and suppliers of Austria; and the poorer they were, the more generous. So much hurt, so much pain, so much sacrifice had gone into making the centre of the Monarchy appear to the eyes of the world as a home of the Graces, of merriment, and genius. Our culture flourished and spread, but their fields were fertilized by sorrow and grief. I thought, while we were sitting together, of Manes

Reisiger and of Joseph Branco. Those two would certainly not go to their deaths as airily, nor die such light-opera deaths as my comrades in my battalion. Nor would I: no, nor would I! Probably in that hour I was the only one who sensed the brute violence of what lay ahead of us, unlike and in contrast to my comrades. Therefore I abruptly got to my feet, and to my own surprise spoke as follows: 'Comrades! You all are dear to me, as should be the situation among comrades in particular in the hour before death.' – And at that point my voice choked. My heart stopped, my tongue faltered. I remembered my father and – God forgive me! – I lied. I put something in the mouth of my late father that he never actually said, though it might have occurred to him to say it. I resumed, then: 'It was one of my father's last wishes that in the event of war, which he correctly predicted, I shouldn't report for duty with my dear Twenty-First, but in the same regiment as my cousin Joseph Branco.'

They fell silent. Never in my life had I heard such silence. It was as though I had spoiled their foolish fun in the war; I was a spoilsport; I had rained on their jolly war.

I distinctly felt I had to go. I rose, and shook hands with everyone. I can still feel the cold, disappointed hands of my Twenty-First. It pained me deeply. But I preferred to die with Joseph Branco, with Joseph Branco, my cousin, the chestnut-roaster, and with Manes Reisiger, the cabbie in Zlotogrod, than with these Viennese waltzers.

So I lost my first home, which was with the Twenty-First, in our beloved 'water-meadows' in the Prater.

# XVI

Now I had to call on Chojnicki's friend, Lieutenant Colonel Stellmacher in the War Ministry. My transfer to the Thirty-Fifth Yeomanry mustn't take any longer than the preparations for my wedding. It suited me to have the two bewildering processes going on in parallel. Perhaps each could put pressure on the other, accelerate it. But both left me stunned, prevented me from finding reasons to justify my haste. At that time all I could think of to say was that 'time was of the essence.' I didn't really want to know why I was in such a hurry. But deep in me, like a sleeper's sense of rain, there was the consciousness that my friends, Joseph Branco and Reisiger, were moving westward along the muddy roads of East Galicia, pursued by Cossacks. Who knows, perhaps they were already wounded or dead? All right, then the most I could do would be to honour their memory by serving in their regiment. How young I was and how little idea we had of war! How easily I fell for the notion that it was my job to tell the good fellows of the Thirty-Fifth part true and part invented stories about their fallen comrades Trotta and Reisiger, so that their names might be remembered. Poor loyal peasants served in the Thirty-Fifth, sergeant-majors with army German grafted over their Slavic mother-tongues like badges sewn on a lapel, or golden yellow seams on tiny dark green fields; and the officers were not the pampered children of our lackadaisical Viennese society, but the sons of craftsmen, postmen, policemen, tenant-farmers and tobacco dealers. To be taken up by them meant as much to me as it would for the likes of them to be transferred to Chojnicki's Ninth Dragoons. It was one of those ideas that people like to dismiss as 'romantic'. Well, far from feeling embarrassed about such a thing, I would today insist that this 'romantic' turn in my life brought me closer to reality than any of the rare occasions when I forced myself to adopt 'realistic' views: how foolish all these dated terms are anyway! And if you insist on them, well, it has always been my experience that the so-called realist stands there rather defensively in the world like a high protective wall of cement, while the so-called romantic is like an open garden, in which truth wanders in and out at will . . .

So I paid my call on Lieutenant-Colonel Stellmacher. In the old Monarchy a transfer from the army to the Yeomanry, or even from the Jägers to the infantry was a bureaucratic procedure just as complicated and certainly more arcane than filling the command of a division. Even so, in that bygone world of mine, of the old Monarchy, there existed certain delicate, exquisite, unwritten, unknown, ungraspable laws familiar only to insiders that were more inviolable and lasting than the written ones that proclaimed that of every hundred petitions, just seven would be answered swiftly, easily and silently in the affirmative. I know that the barbarians of absolute justice are still up in arms about this today. They scold us for aristocrats and aesthetes, even now; and all the time I can see how they, the egalitarians and anti-aesthetes, have prepared the way for their brothers, the barbarians of a stupid and plebeian *in*justice. Absolute justice is a sowing of dragon's teeth.

But just then I had no inclination or leisure to reflect. I went straight to Stellmacher, down the corridor stuffed with patiently waiting Captains, Majors and Colonels, straight through the door that had 'Private. No Entry' on it – me, a wretched little Jäger Ensign. 'Servus!' Sitting hunched over his papers, Stellmacher greeted me, before raising his eyes to see who it was. He knew how familiarly one had to greet people who enter through prohibited doors. I took in his bristly grey hair, the yellowish forehead with its thousand creases, the tiny, deeply buried lidless eyes, the thin bony cheeks and the great drooping, dyed, almost Saracen moustache in which was vested the entire vanity of the man, so that it didn't disturb him otherwise (either in private life or at work). The last time I had seen him was in the Konditorei Demel at five in the afternoon, with Court Councillor Sorgsam from the Ballhausplatz. We hadn't the least intimation of war, and May, the urbane May of Vienna, swam in the little silver-rimmed coffee cups, floated over the place settings, the narrow, stuffed chocolate eclairs, the pink and green pastries that suggested edible jewels, and Count Councillor

Sorgsam gave it as his opinion, smack into the middle of May: 'I tell you, gentlemen, there won't be any war!' And now a harassed looking Stellmacher was looking up from his papers; he didn't see my face to begin with, just uniform, sword knot, sabre, enough to repeat his opening 'Servus!' and thereupon, 'Have a seat, I'll be with you in a moment!' Finally he looked at me closely: 'You're smart!' and 'I almost didn't recognize you! The uniform's made a man of you!' But it wasn't the usual, low sonorous voice of Stellmacher's I'd known for years – even his little joke seemed forced. Never before had a flip word emerged from Stellmacher's mouth. It would have been caught in the glossy hedge of the dyed moustaches, and there silently perished.

Quickly I told him what I'd come for. I also tried to explain why I wanted to join the Thirty-Fifth in particular. 'I only hope you can still find them!' said Stellmacher. 'The news isn't good! Two regiments cut to ribbons, in full retreat. Our idiots of generals had us in such a beautiful state of readiness. But very well. Go, and see if you can find your Thirty-Fifth! Pick up a couple of stars. You'll be transferred as a lieutenant. Servus! Dismiss!' He extended his hand to me across his desk. His light, almost lidless eyes – of which one refused to believe they were ever victim to sleep, drowsiness or even fatigue – fixed me, distantly, strangely, from a glassy distance – by no means sad, no, sadder than sad, in other words hopelessly. He attempted a smile. His big false teeth shimmered in two white rows under the Saracen moustache 'Send me a postcard!' he said, and bent over his papers again.

# XVII

The priests in those days worked as quickly as the bakers, gunsmiths, railway company directors, cap-makers and military outfitters. We were to get married in the church in Döbling; the man who had christened my bride was still alive, and my father-in-law, like most army contractors, was a sentimental johnnie. My bridal present was strictly speaking my mother's. It hadn't occurred to me that presents for the bride were called for. When I arrived for lunch – I'd also forgotten about there being dumplings – my mother was already sitting at table. As ever, I kissed her hand, and she kissed my forehead. I told the man to pick up my dark green cuffs and stars at Urban's in the Tuchlauben. 'Are you being transferred?' asked my mother. 'Yes, Mama, to the Thirty-Fifth!' 'Where are they stationed?' 'In Galicia.' – 'Are you going tomorrow?' 'The day after!' 'The wedding is tomorrow?' 'That's right, Mama!'

In our house the custom at mealtimes was to praise the food, even if it was badly cooked, and not to talk about anything else. Nor should the praise be perfunctory or banal, a certain extravagance was *de rigueur*. So I would say for instance that the meat reminded me of an occasion some six or eight years ago, also a Tuesday, and the cabbage with dill, today as then, was a match made in heaven for the boiled beef. When faced with the plum dumplings I was affected by utter speechlessness. 'Please, more of the same, just like these, the moment I'm back!' I said to Jacques. 'As you say, sir!' replied the old fellow. My mother rose, even before coffee, which was most unusual. She took out of her armoire two dark red morocco leather boxes which I had often had occasion to see and admire and puzzle over, but never dared to ask her about. I had always been curious, but at the same time delighted that there were two sealed mysteries in my proximity.

Now all would be revealed. The smaller box contained an enamel miniature of my father, framed in a thin circlet of gold. His big moustaches, his dark, gleaming, almost fanatical eyes, the heavy, carefully and intricately knotted tie round the strikingly high wing collar made him strange to me. Perhaps that was how he looked before I was born. That was how he was alive and dear and familiar to my mother. I am blond and blue-eyed, my eyes were always sceptical, sad, knowing eyes, never the fanatical eyes of a believer. But my mother said: 'You're exactly like him, take his picture with you!' I thanked her and took it. My mother was a clever, clear-sighted woman. Now it became clear to me that she had never seen me properly. Certainly, she loved me deeply. But she was a woman; she loved the son of her husband, not her child. I was the progeny of her beloved: decisively sprung from his loins; and in some secondary way, the fruit of her womb as well.

She opened the second box. There, bedded on snow white velvet lay a large hexagonal amethyst, clasped in a delicately braided gold chain, which made the stone look coarse, almost crude. It wasn't that it was on a chain, more as though it had got the chain into its possession, and dragged it around everywhere like a weak and submissive female slave. 'For your bride!' said my mother. 'Give it to her today!' I kissed my mother's hand, and slipped the second box into my pocket as well.

Just then our manservant announced visitors, my father-in-law and Elisabeth. 'In the drawing-room,' decreed my mother. 'My mirror!' Jacques brought her the oval hand-mirror. She studied her face in it for a long time, impassively. The women of that time did not need to adjust their dress, complexions or hair by means of make-up, powder, combs, or even by running their fingers through their hair. It was as though my mother was using the mirror to command everything she saw in it – hair, face, dress – to the most punctilious discipline. Without her having raised a finger, all intimacy and closeness suddenly disappeared, and I felt almost like the guest of an elderly lady I didn't know very well. 'Come!' she said. 'My cane!' Her cane, a thin wand of ebony, leaned against her chair. She needed it not for support but as a prop for her dignity.

My father-in-law in a morning-coat and not so much wearing gloves as issued with them, Elisabeth in a high-necked silver-grey dress, a diamond cross on her bosom, looking taller than usual, and as pale as the dull silver clasp at her left hip, were both standing almost rigidly upright as we entered. My father-in-law bowed, Elisabeth performed a slight curtsey. Unbothered, I kissed her. The war rendered all ceremonial obligations superfluous. 'Forgive the ambush!' said my father-in-law. 'You mean the pleasant surprise,' my mother corrected him. She was eyeing Elisabeth as she spoke. Well, in a couple of weeks, I'd be home again, joked my father-in-law. My mother sat bolt upright on a hard, narrow rococo chair. 'People', she said, 'sometimes know when they're leaving. They never know when they're returning.' She eyed Elisabeth. She ordered coffee, cognac and liqueurs. Not for a second did she smile. At a certain moment she looked hard at my tunic pocket, where I had stashed the box with the amethyst. I understood. Without a word, I looped the chain round Elisabeth's neck. The stone hung over the cross. Elisabeth smiled, walked over to the mirror, and my mother nodded at her; Elisabeth took off the cross. The crude purple amethyst shimmered on her silver-grey dress. It looked like frozen blood on frozen ground. I turned away.

We rose. My mother embraced Elisabeth without kissing her. 'Leave now with our visitors!' she told me. 'Come back tonight!' she added. 'I want to know when the wedding is to be. We're having trout, *bleu*!' She waved her hand, as crowned heads wave with their fans. She left the room.

Downstairs, in the car (my father-in-law told me the make, I forgot it), I learned that everything in the Döbling church was ready. The hour was not yet fixed, but would probably be ten o'clock. Our witnesses were Zelinsky and Heidegger. Simple ceremony. 'Martial,' said my father-in-law.

That evening, while we slowly and carefully ate our trout, *bleu*, my mother, probably for the first time since she had taken over the household, started to talk of so-called serious subjects during a meal. I was just launching into praise of the trout. She interrupted me. 'Perhaps this is the last time we will sit together!' she said. Nothing more. 'You'll be going out tonight to say your goodbyes?' 'Yes, Mama!' 'Till tomorrow, then!' She left without turning round.

Yes, I went out to say my goodbyes. Or rather, I wandered around, trying to. Here and there I ran into someone I knew. The people on the pavements blurted out incomprehensible cries. It took me some time before I had understood what they were saying. Bands were playing the Radetzky March, the Deutschmeister March, or *Heil du, mein Österreich*! There were gypsy bands, Heurigen bands, in bourgeois establishments. People were drinking beer. Wherever I walked in, a couple of NCOs would get to their feet to salute, and civilians would wave their beer mugs in my direction. I had the feeling I was the only sober man in the whole city, and that made me feel odd. Yes, my city withdrew from me, moved away from me, further with each passing minute, and the streets and lanes and gardens, however noisy and crowded they were, seemed to me to have died out, just as I would see them later, after the war and after coming home. I wandered around into the small hours, took a room in the old Bristol, had a couple of hours' sleep, wrestling the while with plans and thoughts and memories, went to the

War Ministry, received my confirmation, drove to our old bar-racks on the Landstrasser Hauptstrasse, said goodbye to Major Pauli our commanding officer, received 'open orders' telling me to join the Thirty-Fifth, hurried to Döbling, heard that I was to be married at half past ten, returned to my mother to give her the news, and then to Elisabeth.

We let it be known that Elisabeth would accompany me a ways. My mother kissed me, as per usual, on the forehead, got into her cab quick and cold and brisk, in spite of her slow air. It was a sealed carriage. Even before it started to move, I could see her hurriedly pull down the blinds in the little window in the back. And I knew that within, in the gloom of the little compartment, she was just starting to cry. My father-in-law kissed both of us blithely and cheerily. He had dozens of plat-itudes for the occasion, and they came tumbling out of him, and, like smells, were quickly dispelled. We left him, somewhat brusquely. 'I'll just let you get on with it, then!' he called out after us.

Elisabeth wasn't accompanying me to the East. Rather, we were going to Baden together. We had sixteen hours ahead of us, sixteen long, full, replete, fleeting, inadequate hours.

# XVIII

Sixteen hours! I had been in love with Elisabeth for three years, but those three years struck me as brief compared to the sixteen hours, when surely it should have been the other way around. Forbidden things are rushed, while what is sanctioned has a certain built-in longevity. Besides, while Elisabeth didn't seem changed to me, she seemed at least to be on the way to change. I thought about my father-in-law, and detected similarities between him and her. A few of her hand gestures were clearly his; they were like distant and refined echoes of gestures of her father's. Some of the things she did on the little electric train to Baden almost offended me. For example, barely ten minutes after we had started moving, she took a book out of her little valise. There it was, between her cosmetics bag and her underthings – the bridal robe, I was thinking – and the very fact that a book of all things could presume to rest on such a near-sacramental garment seemed outrageous to me. (The book, incidentally, was a collection of gags of one of those North German humorists who at that time, along with our Nibelung tendency, the German *Schulverein*, and itinerant lecturers from Pomerania, Danzig, Mecklenburg and Königsberg, were just beginning to spread their drizzly good humour and their noisome expansiveness over Vienna.) Elisabeth looked up from her book, looked at me, looked out of the window, stifled a yawn, and went back to her book. She had a way of crossing her legs that struck me as positively indecent. Was she enjoying her book, I asked. 'Funny!' she observed. She passed it to me, so that I might see for myself. I started reading one of the silly tales halfway through; it was about the delicious humour of August the Strong, and a relationship with a cheeky lady-in-waiting. The two epithets, to my mind indicative of Prussian and Saxon souls on their day off, were enough for me. 'Delicious,' I said, 'delicious and cheeky!' Elisabeth smiled, and read on. We had a reservation at the Golden Lion hotel. Our old servant was in attendance, the only person who had been made privy to our Baden plan. He confessed to me right away that he had betrayed it to my mother. He stood there, at the terminus of the electrical suburban line, holding in his hand the stiff bowler hat that my father had probably left him, and presented my wife with a bouquet of dark red roses. He kept his head bowed, the reflection of the sun left a speck of silver on his bald pate, like a little star. Elisabeth was silent. If only she would say something! I thought. Nothing came. The silent ceremony went on for ever. Our two little cases stood together on the pavement. Elisabeth clutched her roses to her, along with her handbag. The old fellow asked us if there was anything he could do for us. He conveyed greetings from my mother. My trunk with my spare uniform and my linens was already in the hotel. 'Thank you!' I said. I observed how Elisabeth flinched and moved a little to the side. This flinching, this desertion provoked me. I told Jacques: 'Accompany us to the hotel, will you! I want to talk to you still.' 'Very good, sir!' he said, and he picked up our cases and toddled off after us.

'I need to have a chat with the old man!' I said to Elisabeth. 'I'll be up in half an hour!'

I went with Jacques to the café. He kept his bowler hat on his lap; gently I took it away from him, and set it on the chair next to us. All of Jacques's tenderness seemed to flow to me from the distant, pale blue, slightly moist old eyes; it was as though my mother had left one last maternal message for me in those eyes. His gouty hands (it was a long time since I had last seen them bare, they were only ever in white gloves) trembled as they picked up his coffee cup. They were good faithful servant's hands. Why had I never looked at them before? Blue knots sat atop the crooked joints of the fingers, the nails were flat, fissured and blunt, the bump of bone at the wrist was askew and seemed unwillingly to suffer the stiff edge of the old-fashioned cuffs, and innumerable pale-blue veins, like tiny rivulets, made their laborious way under the cracked skin of the back of the hand.

We sat in the garden of the Astoria Café. A dry, golden chestnut leaf sailed down and settled on Jacques's bald skull; he didn't feel it, his skin had grown leathery and insensitive; I let the leaf lie. 'How old are you?' I asked him. 'Seventy-eight, young master!' he replied, and I saw a single, large, yellow snaggle-tooth under the thick, white moustache. 'It should be me going to war now, not the youngsters!' he went on. 'I was there in '66, against the Prussians, with the Fifteenth.' 'Where were you born?' I asked. 'In Sipolje!' said Jacques. 'Do you know the Trottas?' 'Of course I do, all of them!' 'And can you still speak Slovene?' 'I've forgotten, young master!'

'Half an hour!' I had told Elisabeth. I was reluctant to take out my watch. More than an hour might have passed, but I couldn't tear myself away from Jacques's pale blue eyes, in which dwelt his pain and my mother's. I felt somehow as though in the space of this single hour I could atone for the past twenty-three years of my facile and loveless life, and instead of embarking on my so-called new life in the traditional manner of a newly-wed, I bent my mind to try to correct the one that was behind me. Ideally, I would have started again with my birth. It was clear to me that I had made a mess of the most important things. Too late. And now I was standing before death and before love. For an instant – I admit – I even considered a scandalous, disgraceful ruse. I could send Elisabeth a message that I had to leave instantly for the Front. Or I could tell it to her face, embrace her, mime the despairing, the inconsolable. It was just a momentary confusion. I got over it right away.

I left the Astoria. Loyally, half a step behind me, went Jacques. Just before the entrance to the hotel, as I was about to turn and say goodbye to him, I heard a faint gurgle. I half-turned and spread my arms. The old fellow slumped against my shoulder.

His bowler hat rolled over the cobbles. The hotel porter came running out. Jacques was unconscious. We carried him into the lobby. I sent for the doctor, and ran up to tell Elisabeth.

She was still sitting over her humorist, drinking tea, and pushing little pieces of buttered toast and jam into her sweet red mouth. She set her book down on the table, and spread her arms. 'Jacques,' I began, 'Jacques . . .' and I faltered. I didn't want to say the terrible verb. A smile of lustfulness and indifference and cheerfulness quivered round Elisabeth's mouth, a smile I thought I would only be able to dispel if I used the macabre word itself — and so I said it: 'He's dying!' She dropped her arms, and said merely: 'He's old!'

People came for me, the doctor was there. The old fellow had been put to bed in his room. His starched shirt had been taken off. It hung over his black jacket, a gleaming linen breast-plate. His polished boots stood like two sentries at the foot of his bed. His woollen socks, multiply darned, lay curled over them. That was all that was left of a simple human being. One or two brass buttons on the bedside table, a collar, a tie, boots, socks, jacket, trousers, shirt. The old feet with their hammer toes peeped out of the end of the bed. 'Heart attack!' said the doctor. He had himself just been called to the colours, a regimental doctor, already in uniform. Tomorrow he was joining the Deutschmeisters. Our formal exchange of greetings at this death-scene was like something from an alternative theatre production, somewhere in Wiener Neustadt. We both felt ashamed. 'Is he going to die?' I asked. 'Is he your father?' asked the doctor. 'Our retainer!' I said. I would rather have concurred:

yes, my father. The doctor seemed to sense it. 'Probably,' he said. 'Tonight?' He shrugged.

All of a sudden it was evening. The lights came on. The doctor gave Jacques an injection of Cardiazol, wrote out prescriptions, rang the bell, sent for someone to go to the apothecary. I slunk out of the room. Just the way a traitor slinks away, I thought. I slunk up the stairs to Elisabeth, as though afraid I might wake someone. Elisabeth's door was locked. My room was the one beside it. I knocked on the door, and then tried it. The connecting door was locked as well. I wondered briefly whether to force it. But at that instant I knew there was no love between us. It seemed I had two fatalities to mourn; and my love was the first to go. I buried it under the threshold of the door between our two rooms. Then I went down a flight of steps to sit with Jacques.

The good doctor was still there. He had unbuckled his sword and unbuttoned his tunic. It smelled of vinegar, ether and camphor in the room, and through the open window streamed the damp, withered air of an autumn evening. The doctor said: 'I'll stay for as long as I'm needed,' and he shook my hand. I sent my mother a telegram, saying that I had need of our retainer, at least until it was time for me to go. We ate ham, cheese and apples. We drank a couple of bottles of Nussdorfer.

The old man lay there, blue in the face, his breathing audible throughout the room like a rasping saw. From time to time his upper body would seize up, and his bent hands would pluck at the dark red quilt. The doctor wet a towel, shook a little vinegar on to it, and laid it on the dying man's forehead. Twice I went upstairs to Elisabeth. The first time, there was silence. The second time I could hear her sobbing loudly. I knocked harder. 'Leave me alone!' she cried. Her voice pierced me through the locked door like a knife.

It was about three in the morning, I was perched on the side of the bed, the doctor, in shirtsleeves, was asleep at the desk, his head in his arms. Then Jacques sat up with arms outstretched, opened his eyes, and babbled something. The doctor straightaway awoke and went to the bed. Then I heard Jacques's old clear voice: 'Please would the young master tell madam I'll be back tomorrow morning.' He fell back into the pillows. His breathing came more quietly. His eyes were fixed and open; it was as though they no longer needed eyelids. 'He's dying,' said the doctor, just as I was deciding to go up to Elisabeth once more.

I waited. Death seemed to approach the old man on stockinged feet, like a father, a true angel. At four in the morning, a breeze blew a yellow, withered chestnut leaf in through the window. I picked it up and laid it on Jacques's quilt. The doctor put his arm round my shoulder, then bent down over the old man to listen, took his hand, and then said: 'Gone'. I knelt down and, for the first time in many, many years, crossed myself.

Not two minutes later, there was a knock on the door. The night porter had a note for me. 'From Madam!' he said. The envelope was barely stuck down, it seemed to open of its own accord. I read a single line: 'Adieu! I've gone home. Elisabeth.' I showed the doctor the note. He read it and looked at me and said: 'I understand.' Then, after a while: 'I'll sort everything out here, with the hotel and the burial and your Mama. I don't leave Vienna for a while. Where are you off to today?' 'I'm headed East!' 'Servus, then!'

I never saw the doctor again, but I never forgot him. Grünhut was his name.

# XIX

I went into battle as a 'seconded officer'. In my initial access of anger, hurt pride, irritation, vengefulness, what do I know, I had crumpled up my wife's note and stuck it in my trouser pocket. Now I took it out, smoothed it out, and read the line over again. It was clear to me that I had sinned against Elisabeth. A little later, it even seemed to me that I had sinned gravely against her. I decided to write to her, and set about getting some paper out of my pack – in those days, we travelled into battle with leather writing-cases; the empty blue sheet reflected my own irritation back to me. It seemed to say everything I wanted to say to Elisabeth, and I wanted to send it off, as smooth and empty as it was. I just signed my name to it. I posted it at the next station we came to. I crumpled Elisabeth's note a second time. And put it back in my pocket.

I was, according to the 'open orders' issued by the War Ministry and signed by Stellmacher, to report directly to the

Thirty-Fifth Yeomanry regiment, wherever they might be met with, without first reporting to the auxiliary local HQ, which, as a result of the recent fighting, had been withdrawn from the dangerous border region into the interior. I saw myself therefore confronted with the tricky task of tracking down my regiment, which must be on a course of continual retreat, somewhere in a village or wood or small town, in a word, in their 'position', which meant more or less an errant individual hoping to encounter his errant fugitive unit. It was an aspect of warfare that had been neglected in manoeuvres.

It was just as well that this problem took up all my attention. I positively fled into it. That way, I didn't have to think about my mother any more, or my wife, or our dead manservant. My train stopped every half hour or so in some tiny insignificant station. We travelled, a first lieutenant and I, in a small matchbox of a compartment for some eighteen hours to Kamionka. Beyond that point, the regular rails were down. There was only a provisional, narrow-gauge train with three tiny uncovered baggage cars that led on to the nearest field command position that might be able – without guarantees, admittedly – to give information about the whereabouts of individual regiments to 'seconded officers'. The little train trundled along. The locomotive driver kept ringing his bell, because great numbers of casualties, on foot and on various farm vehicles, were streaming the other way. I am – as I had occasion then to learn – pretty impervious to shock. So for instance I found the sight of wounded men lying on litters, presumably because their feet or their legs had been shot off, less terrible than that of single soldiers staggering along with flesh wounds, and fresh blood oozing up through the clean white bandages. And with all that, on both sides of the narrow-gauge rail, the tardy crickets were chirruping, because a deceptively warm September afternoon had misled them into thinking that it was summer yet or again. At the field-command post, I happened to run into the padre of the Thirty-Fifth. He was a plump, self-satisfied man of god, in a tight, close-fitting, gleaming surplice. He had got lost on the retreat, he and his batman, his coachman, and his horse and his canvas-covered baggage wagon, where he kept his altar and mass serving gear, as well as a number of fowls, bottles of brandy, hay for his horse, and various other goodies confiscated from farmers. He hailed me like a long-lost friend. He seemed to be afraid of getting lost again, nor could he bring himself to surrender his fowls to the command post where for the past ten days there had been only conserved goods and potatoes to eat. He wasn't especially well-liked there. But he refused to set out at a peradventure or in a proximate direction, whereas for me, thinking of my cousin Joseph Branco and the cabbie Manes Reisiger, anywhere seemed better than waiting. Our Thirty-Fifth, thus the vague reports we had, was stationed some two miles north of Brzezany. So I set out with the field chaplain, his cart and his fowls, with no better map than a hand-drawn sketch.

When we found the Thirty-Fifth, not admittedly north of Brzrezany, but in the hamlet of Strumilce, I reported to the colonel. News of my promotion had already been passed to the regimental adjutant. I asked to see my friends. They came. I asked for them to be put in my platoon. And how they came! I was waiting for them in the office of Warrant Officer Cenower, but they hadn't been informed that it was I who had sent for them. At first, they failed even to recognize me. But the next instant, Manes Reisiger was flinging his arms round my neck, rule book be damned, while my cousin Joseph Branco, from a mixture of astonishment and discipline, stood to attention. He was a Slovene, of course. But Manes Reisiger was a Jewish cabbie from the East, heedless and mindless of any rule book. His beard was so many wild hard knots; the man didn't look uniformed so much as in disguise. I kissed one of the knots in his beard, and threw my other arm around Joseph Branco. I too was forgetting about the army. I was only thinking about the war, and called out maybe ten times in succession, 'You're alive! You're alive! . . .' and Joseph Branco straightaway noticed the wedding ring on my finger, and pointed silently at it. 'Yes,' I said, 'I've got married.' I could feel, I could see that they wanted to hear more about my wedding and my new wife, I went out with them on to the tiny square around the church in Strumilce. But I didn't talk about Elisabeth at all, until suddenly I remembered – how could I have forgotten it – that I had a photograph of her in my wallet. Surely it was the easiest thing to save myself so many words, and just show my friends her picture. I pulled out my wallet, and I looked and looked, and the picture wasn't in it. I began to wonder where I could have lost it or left it, and suddenly I seemed to remember that I had left the picture with my mother, at home. A baffling, yes, an absurd terror gripped me, as though I had ripped up or burned

Elisabeth's picture. 'I can't find it,' I told my friends. Instead of replying, my cousin Joseph Branco took out the picture of his wife from his pocket and showed it to me. She was a fine-looking woman, voluptuous and proud, in Slovene village costume, with a crown of coins over her smooth parted hair, and a tripled chain of the same coins round her neck. Her strong-looking arms were bare, and she had her hands on her hips. 'The mother of my son!' proclaimed Joseph Branco. 'Are you married?' asked Manes the cabbie. 'When the war is over, I will marry her, our son is called Branco, like me. He is ten years old. He is with his grandfather. He can carve beautiful pipes.'

# XX

The days ahead, capacious and fraught with danger, gloomy and lofty and mysterious and opaque, brought at least no prospect of fighting, just further retreats. Two days later, we left Strumilce for Jeziory, and three days after that we were in Pogrody. The Russians were coming after us. We withdrew as far as Krasne-Busk. Probably as a result of lost or delayed orders, we stayed there for longer than the Second Army intended us to. Early one morning, the Russians laid into us. We had no time to dig in. This was the historic battle of Krasne-Busk, in which one third of our regiment was wiped out, and another third taken prisoner.

We were among the prisoners, Joseph Branco, Manes Reisiger and I. That was the ignominious outcome of our first encounter with the foe.

I would like very much at this point to write about the feelings and perspectives of a prisoner of war. But I know how little interest there is in such a subject nowadays. Being a prisoner is bad enough, being the author of prison reminiscences is beyond endurance. People today would hardly understand me if I started writing about freedom and honour, much less about captivity. Nowadays, silence is the better policy. I am writing purely to obtain clarity for myself, and, so to speak, *pro nomine dei*. May He forgive me my sin!

Well, so we were prisoners of war, the whole of our platoon. Joseph Branco and Manes Reisiger and I managed to stay together. We were so to speak birds of a feather. 'The war is over for us,' said Manes Reisiger. 'I've never been taken prisoner before,' he added sometimes, 'no more than you. But I know that life and not death awaits us. You will both remember that when we return. If only I knew what my Ephraim is doing. The war will go on for a long time. My son will join up. Remember! Manes Reisiger from Zlotogrod, an ordinary cabbie, said so!' Whereupon he clacked his tongue, like the crack of a whip. For the next few weeks he did not speak.

On the evening of 2 October we were to be parted. As was the accepted practice in those days, our captors intended to separate the officers from the men. We were all to be held in the interior, but the men were to be shipped much further away. The name Siberia fell. I volunteered for Siberia. To this day I don't know or want to know how Manes Reisiger managed to get me to Siberia. Never, it seems to me, can a man have been so happy to have secured disadvantages for himself by bribery and cunning. All the credit was Manes Reisiger's. From the moment we were taken prisoner, he had assumed command over us, all our platoon. What is there that can't be learned from horses, with the grace of God, if you happen to be a cabbie! And a Jewish one at that, from Zlotogrod . . .

I won't describe the highways and byways by which we got to Siberia. There are always highways and byways. At the end of six months, we found ourselves in Viatka.

# XXI

Viatka is on the river Lena, in the depths of Siberia. The journey there takes half a year. In the course of getting there, we had forgotten the innumerable and identical sequence of days. Who counts the corals on a sixfold chain? Our transport took six months. It was in September that we were taken prisoner, it was March when we reached our destination. In the Augarten in Vienna, the laburnum would be flowering soon; before long the elderflower would spread its scent. Here, vast floes of ice drifted down the river, you could get across it dry-footed, even at its widest point. During our transport three men in our platoon had died of typhoid. Fourteen had tried to run away, six members of our escort had deserted with them. The young Cossack lieutenant who was in command of this latest stage of the transport left us in Chirein: he had to catch both the fugitives and the deserters. Andrei Maximovitch Krassin was his name. On his return, he and I played cards together while his patrols combed the area looking for the absconded men. We spoke French together. He drank the home-distilled *samogonka* brought to him by the rare Russian settlers in the area, out of a pouchy field-flask, and he was personable and grateful for each kind look I gave him. I liked his laugh, the dazzling strong white teeth under the short coal-black moustache, and the eyes that were reduced to sparks when he squeezed them shut. He was a grand master of laughter. I would say to him: 'Won't you laugh for me?' and in a trice – generous, noisy, large-hearted – he would be laughing. One day his patrols caught up with the fugitives. Those that were left, anyway, eight of the original twenty. The rest were either lost or hidden or dead somewhere. Krassin was playing tarock with me in the station building. He summoned the apprehended men, gave them tea and schnapps, and ordered me who was subject to his orders, to determine the punishment both for the members of my platoon, and the two recaptured Russian deserters. I told him I wasn't *au fait* with his army's regulations. First he asked, then he threatened, and finally I said: 'Since I don't know what punishments should be handed down according to your rulebook, it is my decision that all shall remain unpunished.'

He laid his pistol on the table and said: 'This is a conspiracy. I will have you arrested, lieutenant, and taken away!' 'Shouldn't we finish our game first?' I asked, picking up my cards. 'Of course,' he said, and we went on playing, while soldiers, Austrians and escorts milled around us. He lost. I could easily have let him win, but I was concerned lest he might notice. Childlike as he was, suspicion was an even greater source of pleasure to him than laughter, and his readiness to suspect was always there. So I beat him. He knitted his brows and scowled at the NCO in command of the escort as though he was about to order all eight men to be shot. 'Won't you laugh?' I asked. He laughed straightaway, generous, large-hearted, with all his dazzling teeth. I thought I had saved the lives of all eight men.

He laughed for about two minutes, and then suddenly, as was his wont, was serious again, and commanded the NCO: 'I want all eight clapped in irons! Dismiss! Await further instructions.' Then, once the men had left the building, he started to shuffle the cards. 'All right. Payback time.' We played another round. He lost again. At that point he picked up his revolver, got up and walked out, saying: 'I'll be back.' I remained seated; two petroleum lamps were lit. The Karvasian landlady wobbled in, with a new glass of tea. The fresh tea had the same slice of lemon in it. The landlady was as broad in the beam as a tugboat, but she smiled like a good sort, confiding and motherly. When I made to take the old used lemon slice out of the glass, she reached in two of her fat fingers and fished it out for me. I gave her a look of thanks.

I sipped my hot tea. Lieutenant Andrei Maximovitch didn't return. It grew late, and I was due to go back to my men in the camp. I stepped outside, in front of the balcony door, and called Krassin's name a couple of times. At last he answered. The night was so cold that I first thought a shout would shiver to pieces in the air and never reach its intended destination. I looked up at the sky. The silver stars didn't look as though they belonged to it, more as though they were gleaming nails knocked into its canopy. A strong wind out of the East, the tyrant among the Siberian winds, took the breath out of my throat, stopped my heart, and briefly blinded me. The lieutenant's reply to my call, carried to me on that bad wind, struck me as a comforting message from a human being, the first I'd heard for a long time, and that even though I'd only been waiting outside in the hostile night for a few minutes. But then this human message turned out to be anything but comforting.

I went back inside. A single lamp was still burning. It didn't light the room so much as refine its darkness. It was the tiny luminous kernel of a heavy, orbic darkness. I sat down beside the lamp. Suddenly a couple of shots rang out. I ran outside. The shots hadn't finished echoing away. They were still rolling around under the huge, icy sky. I listened. Nothing moved, nothing except the steady arctic wind. I could stand it no longer, and went back inside.

Shortly afterwards, the lieutenant came in, pale, cap in hand in spite of the wind, his pistol half out of its holster.

He sat down right away, breathing hard, unbuttoned his tunic, and looked at me with staring eyes, as though he didn't know me, as though he had forgotten who I was and was straining to identify me. He swept the cards off the table with his sleeve. He took a long pull from his flask, lowered his head, and suddenly, rapidly said: 'I only hit one of them.' 'Poor aim,' I said. But he meant it differently.

'You're right. I aimed badly. I had them form up in a line. I only wanted to give them a fright. I fired into the air. The last shot, it was as though something was pressing my arm down. I don't know how it happened. The man is dead. My men can't understand me any more.'

The soldier was buried that same night. The lieutenant accorded him full military honours. He never laughed again. He was reflecting about something that seemed to be preoccupying him.

We covered another ten versts or so under his command. Two days before the next commander was due to take over from him, he asked me to join him in his sleigh, and said: 'This sleigh now belongs to you and your two friends. The Jew is a coachman, he'll know his business. Here's my map. I marked the point where you get off. You will be expected. The man is a friend of mine. Trustworthy. No one will come after you. I will report all three of you as fugitives. I will shoot you and have you buried.' He pressed my hand, and got out.

That night we set off. The trip was just a couple of hours. The man was there, waiting. We felt right away that we were safe with him. A new life began.

# XXII

Our host belonged to the long-established community of Siberian Poles. He was a trapper by profession. He lived on his own, with a dog of no certifiable breed, a couple of hunting rifles, a number of home-made pipes, in two spacious rooms full of scruffy furs. His name was Baranovich, first name of Jan. He hardly spoke. A full black beard enjoined him to silence. We did all sorts of work for him, repairing his fence, splitting firewood, greasing the runners on his sleigh, sorting furs. These were all useful occupations for us to learn. But even after a week there, it was clear to us that he only allowed us to work for him out of a sense of tact, and so that in the isolation we didn't quarrel with him or each other. He was right. He carved pipes and canes out of the limbs of a tough shrub he called *nastorka*, I don't remember why. He broke in a new pipe every week. I never heard him tell a joke or anecdote. At the most he would take the pipe out of his mouth to smile at one of us. Every two months someone would come from the nearest hamlet, bringing an old Russian newspaper. Baranovich didn't even look at it. I learned a lot from it, but not about the war. Once, I read that the Cossacks were about to invade Silesia. My cousin Joseph Branco believed it, Manes Reisiger didn't. They started to quarrel. For the first time they quarrelled. In the end, they too were in the grip of that madness that is the inevitable outcome of isolation. Joseph Branco, younger and more hot-tempered, grabbed at Reisiger's beard. I was just washing up in the kitchen when it happened. When I heard the quarrel, I dashed into the room, plate in hand. My friends had neither eyes nor ears for me. For the first time, even though I was shocked by the violence of two people I loved, I was struck also by the sudden understanding which came to me: namely the revelation that I was no longer one of them. I stood before them, like a hapless umpire, no longer their friend, and even though I was perfectly sure that a kind of cabin fever had them in its grip, I believed I was somehow immune to it. A kind of hateful indifference filled me. I went back into the kitchen to finish the washing up. They went wild. But, as though I expressly wanted not to disturb them in their crazed fight, in the way that you try not to disturb people when they're asleep, I put the plates down very quietly, one on top of the other, to avoid making the least noise. After I was done, I sat down on the kitchen stool, and waited patiently.

Eventually, they both came out, one after the other. They wouldn't look at me. It seemed each of them separately – seeing as they were now enemies – wanted to make me feel his disapproval because I hadn't intervened in their quarrel. Both turned to some needless task or other. One ground the knives, but it didn't look at all menacing. The other collected snow in a pan, lit a fire, threw in little pieces of kindling, and stared concentratedly into the flames. It got warm. The warmth reached the opposite window, the ice-flowers turning reddish, blue, sometimes violet in the reflection of the blaze. Little ice-patches that had formed on the floor under the leaky window started to melt.

Evening was at hand, the water was bubbling away in the pan. Baranovich was due back from one of his wanderings that he would undertake on certain days, we never knew when or why. He walked in, with his stick in his hand, and his mittens stuck inside his belt. (He had the habit of taking them off outside, a kind of etiquette.) He shook hands with each of us with the familiar greeting: 'God give you health.' Then he took off his fur cap and crossed himself. He walked into the sitting room.

Later, the four of us ate together, as usual. No one spoke. We listened to the hour striking on the cuckoo clock, which made me think of a bird that had lost its way from some other distant country: I was surprised it hadn't frozen. Baranovich, who was used to our customary evening chitchat, looked covertly into each of our faces. At last he got up, not slowly as usual, but suddenly, and seemingly disappointed with us, called 'Good night!' and went into the other room. I cleared the table, and blew out the oil lamp. Night glimmered through the icy panes. We lay down to sleep. 'Good night!' I said, as always. No reply.

In the morning, while I was splitting wood for kindling to

light the samovar, Baranovich came into the kitchen. Unwontedly quickly, he started speaking: 'So there was a fight,' he said. 'I saw the wounds, I heard the silence. I can't keep them here any longer. This house needs to be at peace. I've had guests before. They were always welcome to stay as long as they kept the peace. I never asked anyone where he was from. He could have been a murderer for all I cared. To me he was a guest. I have the watchword: a guest in the house is God in the house. The lieutenant who sent you to me I have known for a long time. I had to throw him out once too for fighting. He wasn't upset. I'd like to keep you. You didn't fight. But the other two will report you. So you'll have to leave as well.' He stopped. I tossed the burning kindling into the samovar pan, and stuffed some loose newspaper over it to keep it from blowing out. When the samovar started to sing, Baranovich resumed: 'You can't run away. In this region, in this season it's impossible for a wanderer to stay alive. There's nothing for you but to go back to Viatka. To Viatka,' he said again, hesitated, and spelled it out: 'to the camp. You may be punished gravely, lightly, or not at all. Then again, there's no shortage of other trouble, the Tsar is far away, his laws are a mess. Report to Sergeant Kumin. He has more power than the camp commandment. I'll give you some tea and makhorka for him. Remember: Kumin.' The water was boiling, I tipped some tea into the chajnik, poured boiling water on it, and put the chajnik on the samovar fire. For the last time! I thought. I wasn't afraid of the camp. It was war, and that's what happened to prisoners: they were put in camps. But I now understood that Baranovich was a sort of father, that I felt at home in his house, and that his bread was the bread of home. The previous day I'd lost my friends. Today I was losing my home. At that time, I didn't realize that it wasn't the last time I would lose my home. The likes of us is marked down by fate.

When I brought the tea in, Reisiger and Joseph Branco were already seated at opposite ends of the table. Baranovich was leaning in the doorway. He didn't sit down, not even when I poured his tea. I cut the bread myself, and doled it out. He stood by the table, drank his tea standing up, standing up he ate his bread. Then he said: 'My friends, I've talked to your lieutenant. It's impossible for me to keep you here any longer. Take your sleigh, stuff a few furs under your coats, they will warm you. I'll take you back to the place where I first met you.'

Manes Reisiger went out; I could hear him towing the sleigh across the crisp snow in the yard. At first Branco didn't realize what was happening. 'All right, let's pack up!' I said. For the first time, I was upset at having to take command.

When we were finished, and were sitting squeezed together in the narrow sleigh, Baranovich said to me: 'Get down, there's something I've forgotten.' We walked back into the house. For the last time, I sneaked a look at kitchen, parlour, window, knife, cutlery, the tied-up dog, the two shotguns, the stacks of furs. My discretion was futile, because Baranovich saw everything. 'Here,' he said, and gave me a revolver. 'Your friends will—' he didn't complete the sentence. I pocketed the revolver. 'Kumin won't search you. Just give him the tea and the makhorka.' I wanted to thank him, but how pitiful thanks would have sounded, thanks from my mouth! It occurred to me how often in my life I had mechanically uttered the word thanks. I had dishallowed it. How hollow it would have sounded to Baranovich's ears, my weightless thank you And even my hand-shake would have been something lightweight – and he was just pulling on his mittens anyway. Only when we got to the place from where he had collected us the first time did he pull off his right mitten, shake our hands, and give us his usual: 'God give you good health!' Then he called out a loud 'Vyo!' to the grey, as though afraid we might stay on the spot. He turned his back on us. It was snowing. He disappeared into the dense whiteness, a ghost in a hurry.

We drove to the camp. Kumin asked no questions. He accepted tea and makhorka and asked no questions. He sepa-rated us. I went to the officers' barracks. I saw Manes and Joseph Branco twice a week during exercise. They never looked at each other. When I sometimes went to one of them to give him a little of my tobacco, whichever of them it was would say, formally and in German: 'Thank you, sir!' 'Everything all right?' 'Yes, sir!' One day at roll call they were both missing. That evening I found a note under my pillow. On it was writ-ten, in Joseph Branco's hand: 'We've gone. We're going to Vienna.'

# XXIII

$\mathbf{A}$ nd Vienna is where I saw them again, four years later.

I got home on Christmas Eve of 1918. The clock on the Westbahnhof showed eleven o'clock. I walked along the Mariahilfer Strasse. A rough sleet, failed snow and wretched brother to hail, slanted down from an inclement sky. My cap was bare, the pips had been torn off it. My collar was bare, the stars had been torn off it. I myself was bare. The stones were bare, and the walls and roofs likewise. Bare the sparse street-lamps. The sleet scrabbled against their dull glass, as though the heavens were chucking handfuls of grit at helpless glass marbles. The coat-tails of the sentries outside the public buildings were flapping, and their skirts bellied out, even though they were sodden. The fixed bayonets didn't look real, the rifles were curled against their shoulders. It was as though the rifles wanted to go to sleep, tired like us from four years of shooting. I wasn't in the least surprised that no one saluted me, my naked cap and naked tunic collar gave no one cause. I wasn't a rebel. I was just a poor wretch. It was the end. I thought of my father's old dream of the triple monarchy, which he had given into my keeping. My father lay buried in the cemetery at Hietzing, and Emperor Franz Joseph, whose dissident loyalist he had been, in the Kapuzinergruft. I was the heir, and the sleet fell on me, and I trudged to the house of my father and mother. I made a detour via the Kapuzinergruft. There too a sentry was going up and down. What did he have to guard? The tomb? The memory? History itself?! I, an heir, stopped in front of the church for a while. The sentry ignored me. I doffed my cap. Then I wandered on, from one house to the next, back to the house of my father. Was my mother still alive? Twice on my way I had sent her word of my return. I walked faster. Was my mother still alive? I stood in front of our house. I rang the bell. I waited a long time. Our old concierge opened the gate. 'Frau Fanny!' I cried. She recognized me right away by my voice. The candle flickered in her hand. 'We're waiting for you, we're waiting for you, young master. We haven't slept for days, neither of us, madam upstairs hasn't neither.' She was indeed dressed as I had only ever seen her on Sunday mornings, never at night after the police curfew hour. I took the stairs two at a time.

My mother stood next to her old chair, in her buttoned-up black dress, her silver hair swept back. Over the crown of two braids lay the broad ridge of her comb, as grey as her hair. The collar and narrow cuffs of her dress were set off by the familiar narrow white lace borders. In conjuration, she raised her old stick with the silver crutch aloft, she raised it to the heavens, as

though her arm alone wasn't enough for the thanks she wanted
to give. She didn't move, she stayed where she was, and her
waiting for me seemed to me like a striding. She bent down
over me. This time she didn't even kiss me on the forehead. She
raised my chin on two of her fingers so that I lifted my face and
saw for the first time that she was much bigger than I was. She
looked at me for a long time. Then something unlikely happened, something alarming, extraordinary, almost unreal: my
mother picked up my hand, bent down, and kissed it twice.
Quickly and in embarrassment I took off my coat. 'The tunic
as well,' she said, 'it's all wet.' I took the tunic off as well. My
mother saw that my right sleeve had a long rip in it. 'Take your
shirt off, I'll sew it for you,' she said. 'No, don't,' I said, 'it's not
clean.' Never could I have dreamed of saying of anything in our
house that it was dirty or soiled. How quickly these ceremonial
usages returned! Only now was I truly back.

I didn't speak, I just watched my mother and ate and drank
the things she had prepared for me, had probably in a hundred
different ways managed to acquire. Lots of things that were
completely unobtainable in Vienna: salted almonds, white
bread, a couple of bars of chocolate, a miniature of cognac, and
proper coffee. She sat down at the piano. It was open. It might
have been like that for days, perhaps since the day I first let her
know I was on my way back. She probably wanted to play some
Chopin for me. She knew that my love of him was one of the
few tastes I had inherited from my father. I could tell from the
thick, yellow, half-burned candles in the bronze candelabra on
the piano that my mother hadn't touched the piano for years.

She once played every evening, only in the evening and only by candlelight. They were still the good stout, almost succulent candles from the old times, nothing like that would have been available during the war. My mother asked me for the matches. There was a matchbox on the mantel. Brown and vulgar as it was, beside the little clock with the delicate girlish face it looked out of place in the room, an intruder. They were sulphur matches, you had to wait a little while their blue flame turned into a healthy, normal one. The smell was intrusive, too. Our living-room had always had a particular smell, a mix of remote, already fading violets, and the bitter spice of fresh, strong coffee. What was sulphur doing here?

My mother placed her dear, old, white hands on the keys. I leaned against her. Her fingers slid over the keys, but there was no sound from the interior of the instrument. It was silent, inert. I couldn't understand. It must be a strange phenomenon; and I didn't understand the first thing about physics. I tried a few notes myself. Nothing. It was ghostly. In curiosity, I lifted the lid of the piano. It was hollow inside: there weren't any strings. 'But it's empty, Mama!' I said. She inclined her head. 'I'd quite forgotten,' she said quietly. 'A few days after you left, I had a strange idea. I wanted to force myself to stop playing. I had the strings removed. I don't know what was going on in my head. I really can't say. I was confused, perhaps even a little unhinged. It's only just come back to me.'

My mother looked at me. There were tears in her eyes, not the flowing kind, but the ones that brim like pools. I threw my arms around her. She patted my head. 'Your hair is full of soot,' she said. She repeated it twice more. 'Your hair is full of soot! Go and wash it!'

'When I go to bed!' I said. 'I don't want to go to bed just yet,' I said, as if I was still a child. 'Let me stay up a bit longer, Mama!'

We sat at the little table in front of the fireplace. 'While I was tidying, I found some cigarettes of yours, two boxes of those Egyptians you liked to smoke. I wrapped them in some damp blotting paper. I'm sure they're perfectly good. Do you want to smoke? They're by the window.'

Yes, they were the old packs of a hundred! I looked at them from all sides. On the lid of one of them I saw, in my hand-writing, almost entirely faded, the name: Friedl Reichner, Hohenstaufengasse. I remembered straightaway. It was the name of an attractive girl who worked in the *Trafik* where I must have bought these cigarettes. The old lady smiled. 'Who is she?' she asked. 'A nice girl, Mama! I never tried to look her up again.' 'And now you're too old', she said, 'to go around picking up girls in *Trafiks*. Anyway, they've stopped making those ciga rettes . . .' It was the first time I'd heard my mother trying herself at a sort of joke.

There was silence for a moment. Then my mother asked me: 'Have you suffered much, boy?' 'Not so very much, Mama.' 'Did you miss your Elisabeth?' (She didn't say: your wife, she said: your Elisabeth, and with the stress on the 'your.') 'No, Mama!' 'Are you still in love with her?' 'Too much water under the bridge, Mama.' 'Don't you even want to ask after her?' 'I was just about to!' 'I've hardly seen her,' said my mother. 'I've seen more of your father-in-law. He was last here a couple of months ago. A little downcast, but still full of plans. He's done well out of the War. They knew you were a prisoner. I think they'd have preferred to see you on the list of casualties, or missing feared dead. Elisabeth . . .' 'It's all right, I can imagine,' I interrupted her.

'No, you can't imagine,' my mother persisted. 'Guess what became of her?'

I tried to think of the worst, or what in my mother's eyes might be the worst thing that could have happened.

'Maybe a dancer?' I suggested.

My mother shook her head solemnly. Then she said slowly, almost grimly: 'No – arts and crafts. Do you even know what that is? She sketches, or who knows, maybe she even carves – these crazy necklaces and rings, those modern gewgaws, you know, all jagged, and brooches of fir. I think she can weave straw carpets too. The last time she was here, she gave me a lecture, like a professor, about African art, I think it was. Once, without asking me, she came with a friend. It was – 'my mother paused for a while before bringing herself to say the word: 'it was one of those hoydens, with short hair.'

'Is that so bad?' I asked.

'It's worse, boy! Once you start making valuable-looking things out of worthless material! Where'll it end? Africans go around in sea-shells, that's another matter. If you cheat people – fine. But these people try to make something virtuous out of the deception. Do you understand, boy? No one can persuade me that cotton is as good as linen, or that you can make laurel wreaths out of pine cones.'

My mother spoke slowly, in her usual quiet tone. Her face flushed.

'Would you have liked a dancer better?'

My mother pondered for a while, then to my great astonishment said:

'Certainly, boy! I wouldn't want a dancer as a daughter-in-law, but at least you know where you are with one. Loose morals are unambiguous. There's no cheating, no deception. The likes of you can have a relationship with a dancer. But an interior designer craves legitimacy and marriage. Now do you see, boy? Once you've got over the war, you will. Anyway, you're to go and see your Elisabeth first thing tomorrow. Where will you live, I wonder? And what will become of you? She's living with her father. What time shall I wake you?'

'I'm not sure, Mama!'

'I breakfast at eight,' she said.

'Then what about seven, Mama!'

'Go to bed, then, boy. Good night!'

I kissed her hand; she kissed me on the forehead. Yes, that was my mother! It was as though nothing had happened, as though I hadn't just come home from the war, as though the world didn't lie in ruins, as though the Monarchy hadn't been destroyed, our old Fatherland with its numerous, baffling but immutable laws, customs, habits, practices, inclinations, virtues and vices still extant. In my mother's house, one got up at seven, even if one hadn't slept for the past four nights. I'd arrived at midnight. Now the old clock on the mantel with its tired, tender girlish face was striking three. Three hours of tenderness were enough for my mother. Or were they? At any rate, she didn't permit another quarter hour. My mother was right; before long I was asleep with the comforting sense that I was home, in the midst of a wrecked Fatherland; I was falling asleep in a fortress. My old mother with her old ebony crutch warded off the confusions.

# XXIV

As yet I wasn't afraid of the new life that was awaiting me; as they nowadays like to say: I hadn't 'clocked' it. Rather, I kept to the little hourly tasks I had to perform; I was like someone standing at the foot of an intimidating flight of stairs, who takes the first one for the most daunting.

We no longer kept a manservant, just a maid. The old janitor did duty for a butler. At nine in the morning, I sent him with flowers and a note to my wife. I announced myself for eleven o'clock, which I thought seemly. I got gussied up, as we used to say. My civilian clothes were as they were. I set off on foot. I was there by quarter to, and killed time in a café opposite. On the dot of eleven, I rang the bell. 'The master and mistress are both out!' I was told. My flowers and note had been delivered. Elisabeth left word that I was to see her in her office in the Wollzeile. So I made for the Wollzeile. A little plate on the door announced: Atelier Elisabeth Trotta. Seeing my name gave me a shock.

My wife greeted me with a 'Servus' and: 'Let's have a look at you then!' I tried to kiss her hand, but she pushed my arm away, which instantly robbed me of my composure. The first woman to push my arm away was my wife! I felt something of the ill-at-ease that always befalls me at the sight of freaks of nature or machines performing human movements: lunatics or herma-phrodites, for instance. But it was Elisabeth all right. She wore a high-necked green blouse with floppy collar and a long masculine tie. Her face was still covered by faint down, I remembered the angle of her neck when she lowered her head, and the nervous drumming of the strong, slender fingers on the table. She was sitting in a bright yellow wooden office chair. In fact, everything here seemed to be bright yellow, the table and a picture frame, and the window surrounds on the large win-dows, and the bare floor. 'You can perch on the table!' she said. 'Help yourself to cigarettes. I'm not completely moved in yet.' And she told me she had built all this up herself. 'With these two hands,' she said, showing me her lovely hands. In the course of the week, the rest of the furniture should arrive, and some orange curtains, who could deny that yellow and orange went together. When she had finished giving her report – she still spoke in her old, hoarse voice that I had loved so much! – she said: 'And what have you been doing with yourself?' 'Oh, I've been here and there.' 'Thank you for the flowers,' she said, 'you sent me flowers – why didn't you telephone?' 'We don't have a phone!' 'Well, tell me all about it!' she commanded, lighting a cigarette. She smoked in a way I've since seen in many other women, the cigarette jammed in the corner of the mouth, and a grimace when they light it, which gives the face the aspect of that paralysis doctors call *facies partialis*, and a hard-won appearance of casualness. 'I'll tell you later, Elisabeth,' I said. 'Whatever you say,' she replied. 'Have a look at my portfolio!' She showed me her designs. 'Very original!' I said. She designed all kinds of things: carpets, shawls, ties, rings, bracelets, light fittings, lampshades. Everything looked somehow jagged. 'Do you understand?' 'No!' 'And how could you!' she said. And looked at me. There was pain in her expression, and I sensed she was thinking of our wedding night. All at once, I felt guilty too. But what could I possibly say? The door flew open, and a dark creature blew in, a gust of wind, a young woman with short black hair and round black eyes, tawny face, and the makings of a moustache over red lips and strong gleaming teeth. The woman roared something into the room that I couldn't understand, I got to my feet, and she sat down on the table. 'This is my husband!' said Elisabeth. A couple of minutes later, I realized that this must be 'Jolanth'. 'Haven't you heard of Jolanth Szatmary, then?' asked my wife. So I discovered that this woman was famous. She was even better than my wife at designing all those things that the arts-and-crafts business seemed to want. I apologized. It was true, neither in Viatka nor on the transports there and back had I come across the name Jolanth Szatmary.

'Where's the old geezer?' asked Jolanth.

'He'll be here soon!' said Elisabeth.

The old geezer was my father-in-law. And soon enough he arrived. He emitted the usual 'Ah!' when he saw me, and embraced me. He was sound and healthy. 'Back in one piece!'

he called out triumphantly, as though he had brought me back himself. 'All's well that ends well,' he added a second later. Both women laughed, and I could feel myself blush. 'Let's have something to eat!' he decreed. 'See this,' he said to me, 'all built up from scratch with my own hands!' And he showed me the hands. Elisabeth pretended to be looking for her coat.

So we went for lunch, or rather drove, seeing as my father-in-law still had his car and driver. 'The usual place!' he ordered. I didn't dare ask what restaurant was his usual place. Well, it was my own stand-by, where my friends and I had eaten so often, one of those old places in Vienna where the maître d' knew the guests better than the waiters who worked for him, and where a diner wasn't a paying customer but a hallowed visitor.

It was all changed. New waiters served us who didn't know me, and who shook hands with my garrulous father-in-law and brought him to his 'special table'. I felt very much a stranger here, stranger than strange. I mean to say, the space was familiar, the walls were my friends, the windows, the smoke-blackened ceiling, the wide green-tiled stove and the blue-rimmed earthenware vase with dried flowers on the windowsill. But strangers served me, and I was seated with strangers at one table eating. I couldn't follow the conversation. My father-in-law, my wife Elisabeth and Jolanth Szatmary were talking about exhibitions; they wanted to start magazines, print posters, attain international fame – what do I know. 'We'll take you on board!' my father-in-law would say to me from time to time; and I had no idea what he wanted to take me on board of. Yes, the very idea of being taken 'on board' pained me.

'Put it on my tab!' called my father-in-law when we were finished. At that instant Leopold turned up behind the bar, Grandpa Leopold as we used to call him. Six years ago we had called him that. 'Grandpa!' I called out, and he emerged. He was probably over seventy now. He walked on trembly legs and those turned-out feet that always give away a long-serving waiter. His pale, red-rimmed eyes behind the wobbly pince-nez identified me straightaway. His toothless mouth broke into a smile, already the white wings of his whiskers spread. He paddled towards me and took my hand tenderly in his, the way you might pick up a bird. 'Oh, I'm so happy you're back, sir!' he crowed. 'Please come again soon. I'll do myself the honour of serving you in person!' And without bothering about the feelings of the clientele, he called out to the landlady at the till: 'A real guest at last!' My father-in-law laughed.

I had to talk to my father-in-law. Now, I thought, I had a view of the whole staircase ahead of me. It had an endless number of steps, getting ever steeper. Of course, I could always abandon Elisabeth and not think about her any more. But I didn't even consider it. She was my wife. (Even today I have the sense that she is my wife.) Possibly I had transgressed against her, certainly I had. Perhaps it was my old, only half-smothered love that was trying to persuade me that it was just a question of my conscience. Perhaps it was my need, the foolish need of all young and halfways young men to take the woman they had once been in love with, then forgotten, and who has now changed, and at any price change her back to what she once was; for reasons of vanity. Well, I had to talk to my father-in-law, and to Elisabeth.

I met my father-in-law in the bar of the hotel where they were bound to remember me. To make absolutely sure, I conducted a little scouting expedition half an hour before. Yes, they were all still with us, two of the waiters had got through unscathed, and the barman too. Yes, they even remembered I had a few debts outstanding – and even that did me good to hear! It was all very calm and peaceful. The light fell sweetly through the glass roof. There were no windows. There were still good old drinks from before the War. When my father-in-law arrived, I ordered cognac. They brought me Napoleon, as of yore. 'What a terror!' said my father-in-law. Well, hardly.

I told him I needed to arrange my life, or rather our lives. I was, I said, not one to put off difficult decisions. I needed to know. I was a man of method.

He listened to me calmly enough. Then he began: 'I'll be perfectly frank with you. First, I have no idea whether Elisabeth still wants to live with you, that is, if she still loves you. That's one thing, and that's for the two of you to work out. Second, what will you live off? Is there anything you can do? Before the War, you were a rich young man from good society, which is the same society my laddie belonged to.'

'My laddie!' He meant my brother-in-law. The one I had never been able to stand. I had completely forgotten about him. 'What's he doing?' I asked. 'He's dead,' replied my father-in-law. He stopped, and drained his glass. 'He fell in 1916,' he added. For the first time he felt like someone I might have some feeling for. 'Anyway,' he went on, 'you don't have money, and you don't have a job. I'm a Commercial Councillor, and even ennobled. Not that that means anything any more. The government owes me hundreds of thousands. They won't pay. All I have is credit, and a little something in the bank. I'm still young. I can get something off the ground. That's what I'm doing right now, as you saw, with the arts and crafts. Elisabeth studied under that renowned Jolanth Szatmary. "Jolanth Studios": with that label, you could export the stuff all over the world. Also' – at this point a dreamy look came into his eye – 'I have a couple more irons in the fire.'

That turn of phrase was enough to put me off him again. He must have sensed it, because he quickly went on: 'Your family is broke, I know that, your mother doesn't. I can get you on board somewhere, if you like. But you need to talk to Elisabeth first. Servus!'

# XXV

So I talked to Elisabeth first. It felt like exhuming something that I had myself consigned to earth. Was there a feeling driving me on, did I have some passion for Elisabeth? I know I was inclined by birth and breeding to take responsibility, and as a strong protest to the new order all round me, where I felt ill at ease, I felt compelled to put some order into my own affairs.

Elisabeth came at the agreed time to the cafe in the city centre where we had once met during the time of my first love for her. I was waiting for her at our old table. Memory, even mawkishness, had me in its grip. I thought the marble table top must still bear traces of our clasped hands. A childish idea, a laughable idea. I knew it, but I forced myself to it, drove myself to it, in a way to be able to supplement my desire to 'put my life in some sort of order' with a measure of emotion, and hence provide a balanced justification for my wanting to talk to Elisabeth. It was at that time that I made the discovery that

our experience is fleeting, our forgetting rapid, and our existence evanescent, as that of no other creature in this world. I
was afraid of Elisabeth; the war, prisoner of war camp, Viatka,
my return were all but extinguished in me. All my experiences
stood in some relation to Elisabeth. And what did she mean,
compared to the loss of my friends, Joseph Branco, Manes
Reisiger, Jan Baranovich, and my home, my world? Elisabeth
wasn't even properly my wife, not in the full bourgeois and
biblical sense of the word. (In the old Monarchy, it would have
been a simple matter for us to get divorced – no doubt even
simpler now.) Did I desire her still? I looked up at the clock.
She would be here in five minutes, and I wished it might be
another half an hour. In my panic I started eating the little
chocolate cakes put together from cinnamon and chicory that
deceive our eyes but cannot take in our palates. (This *Konditorei*
had no schnapps.)

Elisabeth came. She did not come alone. Her friend Jolanth
Szatmary was with her. I had assumed of course that she would
come alone. Now when Jolanth Szatmary turned up as well, I
wasn't even surprised. It was clear to me that Elisabeth would
not, could not, have come without the woman, and I understood.

It wasn't that I was prejudiced, oh no! In the world in which
I had grown up, prejudice was vulgar. To make a public display
of something that was viewed askance didn't seem right to me.
Probably Elisabeth would not have come to our rendezvous
with a woman with whom she was not in love. At this point she
had to obey.

There was an astonishing resemblance between the two of them, even though they were of such different types, and had such utterly different features. It came from the similarity in their clothes and gestures. You might have said they resembled one another like sisters – or like brothers. As men tend to do, they both hesitated outside the door, to see which of them would agree to go in first. There was another hesitation at the table, to see which of them would sit down first. I didn't even try to kiss their hands. I was a ridiculous thing in their eyes, the sprog of a wretched sex, an alien, unimpressive race, unworthy all my life of receiving the distinctions of the caste to which they belonged, or of being inducted in their mysteries. I was still caught in the wicked belief that they belonged to a weak, even a lesser sex, and impertinent enough to try and express this view through gallantry. They sat next to me resolute and contained, as though I had challenged them. Between them there was a silent but perfectly apparent bond against me. It was clearly visible. I made some bland remark, and they exchanged glances, like two who had long known my type, and the sort of things I was capable of saying. Sometimes one of them would smile, and then a split second later, the same smile would appear on the lips of the other. From time to time I thought I noticed Elisabeth incline towards me, try to send me a secret look, as though to show me that she really belonged to me, only to be compelled, against her own will and inclination, to obey her friend. What was there to talk about? I asked her about her work. I got a lecture in return about the reluctance of Europe to appreciate the materials, intentions and genius of the primitive. It was essential to reroute the whole misguided taste of the European in art, and return it to nature. Ornaments were, I was given to understand, useful. I didn't question what I was told. I freely conceded that European taste in arts was misguided. Only I couldn't understand how this aberrant taste had caused the end of the world: wasn't it a consequence, or at any rate a symptom?

'Symptom!' exclaimed Jolanth. 'Didn't I tell you right away, Elisabeth, that he's a blue-eyed optimist! Didn't I recognize it immediately?' With that, she put her small stubby hands on Elisabeth's hand. As she did so, Jolanth's gloves slipped from her lap onto the floor, I stooped to pick them up, but she pushed me away with some force. 'Forgive me,' I said, 'it's the optimist in me.'

'You and your symptoms!' she exclaimed. It was clear to me that she didn't understand the word.

'At eight o'clock Harufax is giving a talk on voluntary sterilisation,' said Jolanth. 'Don't forget, Elisabeth! It's already seven.'

'I'll remember,' said Elisabeth.

Jolanth got up, shooting a glance at Elisabeth to follow her. 'Excuse me!' said Elisabeth. Obediently she followed Jolanth to the lavatory.

They were gone for a couple of minutes. Time enough for me to register that with my insistence on 'putting my life in order', I was only adding to my confusion. Not only was I growing more bewildered myself, I was adding to the general bewilderment. That was as far as I'd got with my pondering when the women came back. They paid. I didn't even manage to call the waitress. Afraid I might anticipate them and curtail their independence, they had, so to speak, nobbled her on the short walk from the toilet to the till. As we said goodbye, Elisabeth pressed a little rolled-up piece of paper into my hand. And then they were off to Harufax, and sterilization. I unrolled the piece of paper. 'Ten at night, Café Museum, alone,' it said. The confusion wasn't over.

The café stank of carbide, or if you prefer, of rotting onions and corpses. There was no electric light. I always find it difficult to concentrate in the presence of strong smells. Smell is a stronger sense than hearing. I waited dully, without the least inclination to see Elisabeth again. Nor did I much feel like 'putting things in order'. It seemed to have taken the carbide to make me see the perverse hopelessness of my desire to make order. I only hung on out of gallantry. But even that couldn't outlast the police curfew. Which in turn – something I would ordinarily have railed against – struck me as excessively generous. The authorities knew what they were doing all right. They were compelling us to drop our inappropriate habits, and to amend our hopeless misunderstandings. But then, half an hour before closing time, Elisabeth arrived. She looked ravishing, storming in, like a hunted animal in her half-length beaver jacket, with snow in her hair and her long lashes, and flakes of snow melting on her cheeks. She looked like something running out of the woods for refuge. 'I told Jolanth that Papa was unwell,' she began. And already there were tears in her eyes. She began to sob. Yes, even though she had on a man's collar and tie under her open fur jacket, she was sobbing. Carefully I took her hand and kissed it. Elisabeth was no longer in any mood to push away my arm. The waiter came along, already out on his feet. Only two of the carbide lamps were still burning. I thought she would order a liqueur, but no, she ordered a pair of frankfurters with horseradish. Nothing gives a woman an appetite like crying, I thought. Anyway, the horseradish would be a cover for her tears. Her appetite moved me. I was overtaken by tender-ness, the mindless, fatal tenderness of the male. I put my arm round her shoulder. She leaned back, dunking her sausage in the horseradish with one hand. Her tears were still flowing, but they meant just as little as the melting snow in her beaver coat. 'I'm your wife, after all,' she sighed. It sounded like a yelp. 'Of course you are,' I replied. Suddenly she sat up straight. She ordered another pair of frankfurters with horseradish and, this time a glass of beer.

Since the second-last carbide lamp was being put out, we had to try to leave. 'Jolanth is waiting for me,' Elisabeth said outside the café. 'I'll walk you,' I said. We walked silently side by side. An inconstant, mouldering snow fell. The streetlamps failed, they too mouldering. They kept a little grain of light in their glass bulbs, spiteful and miserly. They didn't brighten the streets, they darkened them.

When we got to Jolanth Szatmary's house, Elisabeth said: 'Here we are, goodbye!' I took my leave. I asked when I could visit. I made to turn for home. Suddenly Elisabeth put out both her hands towards me. 'Don't leave me,' she said, 'I'll go with you.'

So I took her with me. I couldn't take Elisabeth into any of those houses where I might still be remembered from pre-War times. We were adrift in the great, orphaned, gloomy city, two orphans ourselves. Elisabeth clasped my arm. I could feel her pulse through her fur coat. Sometimes we stopped under one of the miserable lamp posts, and I would look at her wet face. I didn't know if it was from snow or tears.

Somehow we had reached Franz-Josefs-Kai, without knowing it. Without knowing it, we crossed the Augarten bridge. It was still snowing, that ugly, mouldy snow, and we didn't speak. A tiny star blinked at us from a house on the Untere Augartenstrasse. We both knew what the star signified. We went towards it.

The walls were a toxic green, as usual. There were no lights. The porter lit a candle, dribbled a little wax, and gummed it down on the bedside table. A towel hung over the basin. On it was a perfectly round wreath picked out in green thread with a '*Grüss Gott!*' in the middle, in red.

That night, in that room, I made love to Elisabeth. 'I'm a prisoner,' she said to me, 'Jolanth has taken me prisoner. I should never have left, that night in Baden, when Jacques died.'

'You're no one's prisoner,' I replied. 'You're with me, you're my wife.'

I tried to discover all the secrets of her body, and they were many. A youthful ambition – at the time I thought it was masculine – prompted me to wipe out any traces that Jolanth might have left. Was it ambition? Or jealousy?

Slowly the winter morning crept up the toxic green walls. Elisabeth awoke me. She looked very different, looking at me.

With terror in her eyes and reproach; yes, there was a measure of reproach in her eyes. Her stern tie, silvery-grey, hung like a little sword over the arm of the chair. She kissed my eyes sweetly, then she jumped up and shrieked: 'Jolanth!'

We got dressed hurriedly, with an indescribable feeling of shame. The morning was unspeakable. It was raining little hail-stones. We had a long way to walk. The trams weren't yet running. For fully an hour we walked in the teeth of the sleet to Elisabeth's house. She brushed off her gloves. Her hand was cold. 'Goodbye!' I called out after her. This time, she didn't turn round.

# XXVI

It was eight o'clock. My mother was breakfasting, as on any other day. Ritual greetings were exchanged. 'Good morning, Mama!' Today my mother surprised me with a 'Servus, laddie!' It was a long time since I had last heard that boisterous greeting from her lips. When would she have used it last? Maybe ten or fifteen years ago, when I was a schoolboy, in the holidays, when I could stop in for breakfast. At that time she liked to follow that with the anodyne joke that struck her as rather witty. Pointing to the chair I was sitting on, she would ask: 'Well, and is the school bench pinching you?' On one occasion I answered, 'Yes, Mama!' and my punishment was that for three days I wasn't allowed to sit at the table with her.

Today, she even allowed herself a complaint about the jam. 'What I don't understand is where they get all those confounded beets from! Try it, boy! They claim it's oh-so-good for you ...' I ate beets and margarine and drank coffee. The coffee was

130

good. I noticed that our maid poured mine from a different pot, and I saw that the old lady kept the good, hard-to-come-by Meinl coffee for me, and contented herself with bitter chicory brew. But I couldn't let on that I knew. My mother didn't like it when her little tactical moves were seen through. Her vanity was such that she could even cut up on occasion.

'So, you've seen your Elisabeth,' she began abruptly. 'I know, your father-in-law was here yesterday. If I concentrate, I can understand what he says. He was here for a good two hours. He told me you'd spoken to him. I said I was happy to wait to hear about it from you, but there was no stopping him. So, you want to put your life in order – that's what I hear. And what does Elisabeth say?'

'I've been with her.'

'Where? Why didn't you bring her back?'

'I didn't know, Mama. Besides, it was very late.'

'He wants to get you on board somewhere, he said. You have no skills. You can't keep a wife. I don't know where he thinks he's going to get you on board; you'd have to bring some capital with you. And we have nothing. Everything went into those war bonds. So it's lost, just like the war. This house is all we have left. We could take out a loan on it, he said. You might talk to Dr Kiniower about it. But where are you going to work, and what will you do? Do you even know the first thing about arts and crafts? Your father-in-law seems quite the expert. His lecture about it was more exhaustive than your Elisabeth's. And who is Professor Jolanth Keczkemet anyway?'

'Szatmary, Mama!' I corrected her.

'Szekely for all I care,' my mother retorted. 'So who is she?'

'She has short hair, Mama, and I don't like her.'

'And Elisabeth is a friend of hers?'

'A very close friend!'

'Very close, you say?'

'Yes, Mama!'

'Ah!' she said. 'Then leave her be, boy. I've heard about friend-ships like that. I know. I've read things in books, boy. You have no idea how much I know; a boyfriend would have been better. A woman is practically impossible to get rid of. And since when have there been lady professors anyway? What faculty is she in, this Keczkemet?'

'Szatmary, Mama!' I corrected her.

'Have it your own way: Lakatos,' said my mother, on reflec-tion. 'How are you going to compete with a lady professor, boy? A wrestler or an actor would be something else!'

How poorly I had known my mother. The old lady who went to the park once a week to 'take the air' for two hours at a time, and for the same purpose took a cab to the Praterspitz every month, was fully informed about so-called inverts. What a lot she must have read, how clearly she must have reflected and thought about it in the long and lonely hours she spent at home, propped on her black cane, wandering from one of our dimly lit rooms to the next, so lonely and so rich, so sheltered and so knowledgeable, so remote and so worldly wise! But I had to defend Elisabeth – what would my mother think if I didn't! She was my wife, I had just come from our embrace, I could still feel the smooth weight of her young breasts in the palms of my hands, still breathe the scent of her body, the image of her features with the blissful half-closed eyes still lived in mine, and on my mouth was pressed the seal of her lips. I had to stand up for her – and as I defended her, I fell in love with her all over again.

'Professor Szatmary', I said, 'doesn't stand a chance against me. Elisabeth loves me, I am certain of that. Last night, for example . . .'

My mother didn't let me finish: 'And today?' she interrupted me. 'Today she's back with Professor Halaszy!'

'Szatmary, Mama!'

'I don't care what she's called, boy, you know that perfectly well, stop correcting me the whole time! If you want to live with Elisabeth, you'll have to keep her. So, as your father-in-law says, you'll have to take out a loan against our house. What am I saying our house – it's your house! Then that professor with the bloody name will have to go back to making corals out of pine cones – for the love of God! The flat on the ground floor is empty, four rooms, I think, the janitor will know. I have something in the bank, I'll share it with you, ask Dr Kiniower how much there is! And we can share the household. Can Elisabeth cook?'

'I don't believe so, Mama!'

'I used to be able to,' said my mother. 'I expect I can still do some things! But the main thing is that you can live with Elisabeth. And she with you.' She'd stopped saying: your Elisabeth, I took it for a sign of exceptional maternal grace.

'Go out on the town, boy. See your friends! Maybe they're still alive. How about that? A trip to town?'

'Yes, Mama!' I said, and I went to Stellmacher in the War Ministry to ask after my friends. Stellmacher ought to be still extant. Even if the War Ministry was now just a Department. Stellmacher was bound to be around still.

He was – old, stooped and iron-grey. He sat there, behind his old desk, in his old office. But he was in civilian clothes, in a strange, baggy suit which was much too big for him and had been turned. From time to time he drove a couple of fingers down between his neck and collar. His collar bothered him. His shirt-cuffs bothered him. He kept ramming them against the edge of his desk to push them back. He had some information, though: Chojnicki was still alive, and living in the Wieden; Dvorak, Szechenyi, Hallersberg, Lichtenthal and Strohhofer got together every day to play chess in the Café Josefinum on the Währinger Strasse. Stejskal, Halasz and Grünberger were unaccounted for. I went round to Chojnicki's in the Wieden.

He was sitting in his old drawing room, in his old flat, but he was almost unrecognizable, because he had had his moustache taken off. 'Why, whatever for?' I asked him. 'So that I can look like my own manservant. I am my own valet. I open the door to let myself in. I polish my own shoes. I ring when I want something, and then I inquire: what would sir like? Cigarettes! Very good, sir. And I send myself round to the *Trafik*. I can still eat for nothing at the old lady's.' The old lady, in our circle, meant Frau Sacher. 'I still get wine at Fatso's.' Fatso in our circle was Lautgartner in Hietzing. 'And Xandl's lost his marbles and is in the Steinhof,' and with that Chojnicki closed his *tour d'horizon*.

'Lost them?'

'Utterly. I look him up every week. The crocodile'— the uncle of the Chojnicki brothers, Sapieha — 'slapped a court order on the estates. He's Xandl's guardian. I have no say whatever. This flat has been sold. I have another three weeks here. What about you, Trotta?'

'I'm about to mortgage our house. I'm married, you know. I have a wife to feed.' 'Uh-oh, married!' exclaimed Chojnicki. 'Come to think of it, so am I. But my wife is in Poland, God save and protect her, and give her a long life. I decided', he went on, 'to leave everything in the hands of the Almighty. He made my bed, let Him lie in it.' He was silent for a while, then he smashed his fist on the table, and shouted: 'It's you that's to blame for everything, you'— he groped for a word — 'you smart alecs,' he finally said, 'you wrecked our state with your stupid witticisms. My Xandl saw it coming. You failed to see that those Alpine goiters and those Sudeten Czechs, those Nibelung cretins, offended and attacked our nationalities for so long until they began to hate the Monarchy and turned against it. It wasn't our Czechs or our Serbs or our Poles or our Ruthenians who committed treason, but our Germans, our core people.'

'But my family's Slovene!' I said.

'Forgive me,' he replied quietly. 'It's just that I have no Germans here to address myself to. Get me a Sudeten German!' he suddenly yelled, 'and I'll break his neck! Let's go find one! Come on! We're going to the Josefinum!'

Dvorak, Szechenyi, Hallersberg, Lichtenthal and Strohhofer were sitting there, most of them still in uniform. They all belonged to our old group. Aristocratic titles were banned now, but what difference did it make? 'No one who doesn't use my first name', said Szechenyi, 'is worth talking to anyway!' They played chess endlessly. 'All right, where's the Sudeten German?' yelled Chojnicki. 'Here I am!' came the reply, from one of the kibitzers. Papa Kunz, old Social Democrat, editor of the Party newspaper and ready at any moment to prove historically that the Austrians were actually Germans. 'Your proof, sir!' called Szechenyi. Papa Kunz ordered a double slivovitz and embarked on his proof. No one listened to him. 'God damn the Sudetens!' cried Chojnicki, who had just lost a game. He jumped up and ran up to old Papa Kunz with raised, clenched fists. We managed to restrain him. He was foaming at the mouth, his eyes were bloodshot. 'Pruzzian blockheads!' he yelled finally. That was the height of his rage. After that he became visibly milder.

It felt good to be home again. All of us had lost name and rank and station, house and money and net worth, past, present and to come. In the morning when we woke up, and at night when we went to bed, we cursed Death, who had invited us to his great gala celebration. Every one of us envied the fallen. They were resting under the ground, and in springtime violets would sprout from their bones. Whereas we had returned home incurably infertile, with paralysed loins, a doomed race, scorned by Death. The verdict of the military panel was irrevocable and final. It read: 'Found unfit for death.'

# XXVII

We all got used to the unusual. It was a hurried process of adjustment. Not really knowing what we were doing, we hurried to adjust, we chased after phenomena we hated and despised. We began to fall in love with our misery, just as one can love loyal enemies. We buried ourselves in it. We were grateful to it for consuming our little individual personal troubles, like their big brother, proof against consolation, but equally beyond the reach of our little daily anxieties. It is my view that the terrifying meekness of people nowadays in the face of their even worse oppressors is understandable and even to some extent pardonable, if one considers that it's in human nature to prefer the vast, omnivorous misfortune to the specific individual mishap. The outsize calamity gobbles up the little misfortune, the stroke of bad luck. And so we in those years came to love our monstrous misery.

Not, please understand, that we weren't able to redeem a few little joys in the face of it, ransom or reprieve or rescue them. We laughed and joked. We spent money, money that we couldn't in fairness claim was ours – but then it didn't have much value left either. We were happy to borrow it and lend it out, accept it and give it away, ourselves remain in debt, and pay the debts of others. It is like this that mankind will live on the day before the Day of Judgement. Sucking nectar from poisonous flowers, praising the fading sun as the giver of life, kissing the bleaching earth as mother of fruitfulness.

Spring was at hand, the Viennese spring, that none of the sentimental chansons could begin to do justice to. Not one of the popular tunes has the urgency of a blackbird's song in the Votivpark or the Volksgarten. No rhymed strophes are as eloquent as the adorably rough cry of a barker outside a Prater booth in April. Who can sing the careful gold of the laburnum, trying vainly to conceal itself among the alert green of the other shrubbery? The sweet scent of elderflower was approaching, a solemn promise. In the Vienna woods, the violets were out. Young people paired off. In our regular café, we cracked jokes, played chess and dardel and tarock. We lost and won valueless money.

So important was spring to my mother that, from April 15, she redoubled the number of her excursions, and drove out to the Prater twice a month, not once as in winter. There were not many cabs left. The horses died of old age. Many more were slaughtered and made into sausages. In the storehouses of the old army, you could see parts of wrecked hackney cabs. Rubber-tyred carriages that may once have conveyed the Tschirschkys,

the Pallavicinis, the Sternbergs, the Esterhazys, the Dietrich-
steins, the Trautmannsdorffs. My mother, cautious by nature,
and grown more so over the years, had come to an 'arrange-
ment' with one of the few remaining cabbies. He would come
for her punctually twice a month, at nine in the morning.
Sometimes I went with her, especially on rainy days. She didn't
like to be alone in adversity – and rain already counted as such.
We didn't speak much in the quiet penumbra under the rain
roof. 'Xaver,' my mother would say to the cabbie, 'talk to me.'
He would turn to face us, give the horses their heads for a
couple of minutes, and tell us all sorts of things. 'According to
my son,' Xaver told us, 'Capitalism is finished. He doesn't call
me Dad any more. He calls me: Let's go, your Graces! He's a
sharp cookie. He knows what he wants. He doesn't understand
the first thing about horses.' Was she a capitalist, asked my
mother. 'To be sure, ma'am,' replied the cabbie, 'all those that
don't work and that still manage to live are capitalists.' 'What
about the beggars?' asked my mother. 'They might not work,
but then they don't go on excursions to the Praterspitz like you,
ma'am!' replied Xaver. My mother whispered 'A Jacobin!' to
me. She thought she had spoken in the code of the owning
classes. But Xaver understood. He turned round and said: 'It's
my son who's the Jacobin.' Thereupon he cracked his whip. It
was as though he had applauded his own remark, with its
historical culture.

My mother grew more reactionary by the day, especially the
day I took out the mortgage on the house. Arts and crafts,
Elisabeth, the lady professor, short hair, Czechs, Social

Democrats, Jacobins, Jews, tinned meat, paper money, the stock exchange, my father-in-law – all these came in for her contempt and her vitriol. Our solicitor, Dr Kiniower, who had been a friend of my father's, was now called, for simplicity's sake: the Jew. Our maid was the Jacobine. The janitor was a sans-culotte, and Frau Jolanth Szatmary went by Keczkemet. A new personality turned up in our lives, one Kurt von Stettenheim, come all the way from Brandenburg and determined to bring arts and crafts to a waiting world. He looked like one of those men that these days pass for well-bred. By that I mean a mixture of champion tennis player and landowner from no fixed province, with a little maritime whiff of shipping magnate thrown in. Such men may come from anywhere: the Baltic, or Pomerania, or even the Lüneburg Heath. We were relatively lucky with ours: Herr von Stettenheim came from Brandenburg.

He was tall and sinewy, blond and freckled, he wore the inevitable duelling scar on his forehead, the sign of the Borussian fraternity and affected the monocle so anything other than indispensable that we had no option but to call it indispensable. I myself use a monocle on occasion for the sake of convenience, as I'm too vain to wear glasses. But there are certain faces – faces from Pomerania, from the Baltic, from Brandenburg – in which a monocle gives the appearance of being a superfluous third eye, not an aid to vision, but a sort of glass mask. When Herr von Stettenheim screwed in his monocle, he looked like Professor Jolanth Szatmary when she was lighting a cigarette. When Herr von Stettenheim spoke, and much more when he waxed wrathful, then the Cain's mark on his forehead turned blood red – and the man got excited over everything and nothing. There was a perplexing contrast between his zeal and the words in which he expressed it, as for instance: 'Well, I can tell you, I was gobsmacked,' or 'I can only advise you: nil desperandum,' or 'I'll lay ten to one, and shake on it!' And more of the same. Evidently our mortgage wasn't enough for my father-in-law. Herr von Stettenheim promised to invest heavily in the Elisabeth Trotta Studios. Once or twice my father-in-law brought us together. After all, because of the mortgage, he'd now 'taken me on board,' as promised, in the arts and crafts industry. So he had to at least introduce me to the third member of our board. 'I know a Count Trotta!' exclaimed Herr von Stettenheim after we'd barely exchanged two sentences. 'You must be mistaken,' I said, 'there are only Trottas raised to the barony – if indeed they are still alive!' 'I remember now, he was a baron, the old Colonel.' 'You're mistaken again,' I said, 'my uncle is District Commissioner.' 'So sorry!' replied Herr von Stettenheim. And his scar flushed purple.

Herr von Stettenheim had the idea of calling our firm 'Jolan Workshops.' And that was duly how it appeared in the company register. Elisabeth was drawing busily whenever I turned up in the office. She sketched baffling things, for instance nine-pointed stars on the walls of an octahedron or a ten-fingered hand executed in agate, to be called 'Krishnamurti's Benediction', or a red bull on a black ground, called 'Apis', a ship with three banks of oars by the name of 'Salamis', and a snake-bracelet that went by 'Cleopatra'. It was Professor Jolanth

Szatmary who came up with the original ideas, and gave them to her to block out. Apart from that, there were the usual oppressive, hate-filled conventions of cordiality, all overlying our mutual resentment. Elisabeth loved me, of that I was certain, but she was afraid of Professor Szatmary, one of those fears that modern medicine likes to label and is helpless to explain. Ever since Herr von Stettenheim had joined the 'Jolan-Workshops' as co-owner, my father-in-law and the Professor viewed me as a nuisance, a bump on the road to arts and crafts, capable of no useful labour and wholly unworthy of being made privy to the artistic and financial plans of the firm. I was just Elisabeth's other half.

Herr von Stettenheim drew up prospectuses in many world languages, and sent them out in all directions. The fewer the replies, the more furious his zeal. The new curtains came in, two lemon yellow chairs, a sofa, ditto, with black and white zebra stripes, two lamps with hexagonal shades of Japanese paper, and a parchment map on which all cities and countries were marked by drawing pins – all of them, even the ones our company didn't supply.

On evenings when I came to collect Elisabeth, we wouldn't talk about Stettenheim or Jolanth Szatmary or arts and crafts. That was agreed between us. We spent sweet, full spring nights together. There was no doubt about it: Elisabeth loved me.

I was patient. I waited. I waited for the moment when she would tell me of her own volition that she wanted to be all mine. Our flat on the ground floor waited.

My mother never asked me about Elisabeth's intentions.

From time to time she would drop a hint, as for instance: 'Once you've moved in,' or 'when we're all living under the same roof,' and suchlike.

At the end of summer, it turned out that our 'Jolan-Workshops' were not bringing in any money whatsoever. Moreover, my father-in-law hadn't had any luck with his 'other irons'. On the advice of Herr von Stettenheim, he had taken a punt on the Deutschmark. The Deutschmark fell. I was to take out a second, much larger, mortgage on our house. I discussed it with my mother, who didn't want to know. I talked to my father-in-law. 'You're useless, I always knew it,' he said. 'I'll have to have a word with her myself.'

He went to my mother, not alone, but in the company of Herr von Stettenheim. My mother, who was intimidated, sometimes even intolerant of strangers, asked me to wait. I stayed at home. The miracle happened; my mother took to Herr von Stettenheim. During the negotiations in our drawing room, I even thought I saw her leaning forward ever so slightly, to catch his abundant and superfluous speech more clearly. 'Charming!' was my mother's verdict. 'Charming!' she said once or twice more, in response to perfectly ordinary remarks from Herr von Stettenheim. He too – it was his turn – gave a lecture on arts and crafts in general, and the products of the 'Jolan-Workshops, Ltd' in particular. And my dear old mother, who surely understood no more about arts and crafts now than she had a long time ago from hearing Elisabeth discuss them, kept saying: 'Now I understand, now I understand, now I understand!'

Herr von Stettenheim had the good manners to say, 'Columbus's egg, ma'am!' And like an obedient echo, my mother repeated: 'Columbus's egg! We'll take out a second mortgage.'

To begin with, our lawyer Kiniower was against it. 'I warn you!' he said. 'It's a hopeless business. Your father-in-law, I happen to know, has no money left. I've made inquiries. That Herr von Stettenheim is living on the money you are managing to raise. He claims to have a share in Tattersall in the Berlin Tiergarten. My colleague in Berlin informs me that is not the case. As truly as I was a friend to your late lamented Papa: I speak the truth. Frau Jolanth Szatmary is as little a professor as I am. She has never studied at any of the academies in Vienna or Budapest. I warn you, Herr Trotta, I warn you.'

The 'Jew' had little black watering eyes behind a skewed pince-nez. One side of his grey moustache was jauntily curled up, the other dangled despondently down. It looked like an expression of a divided nature. And indeed, he was capable of ending a long, gloomy conversation full of talk of my imminent financial doom, with the cry: 'But everything will turn out for the best! God is a father.' That was a sentence he liked to repeat in any difficult circumstances. This grandson of Abraham, heir to a blessing and a curse, frivolous as an Austrian, melancholy as a Jew, full of emotion but only to the point where emotion can become a danger to oneself, clear-sighted in spite of his wobbly and crooked pince-nez, had over time become as dear to me as a brother. I often dropped in on him in his office, for no particular reason or occasion. On his desk he had photographs of his two sons. The elder had fallen in the war. The younger was studying medicine. 'His head is full of social non-sense!' complained Dr Kiniower. 'How much more important a cure for cancer would be! I'm afraid I'm maybe getting one myself, here, on the kidney! If I have a medical student for a son, then he should be thinking of his old father, and not of saving the world. Enough with saviour already! But you're about to save the arts and crafts! Your Mama wanted to save the Fatherland. She put her fortune in war bonds. There's nothing left but a paltry insurance policy. Your Mama probably imagines it's enough for a ripe old age. She'll get through it in a couple of months, I'm telling you. You don't have a job. Probably you'll never have a job. But unless you start earning money, you've had it. My advice to you is: you have a house, take paying guests. Try and make your Mama understand. This mortgage won't be the last, I'm sure of that. You'll be wanting a third, and then a fourth. Believe me! God is a father!'

Herr von Stettenheim called regularly on my mother, rarely announcing himself in advance. My mother received him warmly, sometimes even rapturously. With grief and aston-ishment I watched as the old, stern and pampered lady indulged his coarse witticisms, his tawdry expressions, his catchpenny gestures, and approved, praised and relished them. Herr von Stettenheim was in the habit of bringing his left wrist up to his eye to look at his watch, with a terrifying abrupt movement of his elbow. Each time he did it, I imagined him poking a neighbour in the eye. His way of extending the pinkie of his right hand when he picked up his coffee cup – that finger on which he wore his great lunk of a seal ring, with a seal that resembled some sort of insect – reminded me of a governess. He spoke in that guttural Prussian that sounds as though it's coming out of a chimney instead of someone's throat, and seems to hollow out even the occasional words of importance that he said.

And that was the man my dear old Mama had fallen for. 'Charming!' she called him.

# XXVIII

He gradually made an impression on me too, though to begin with I failed to notice. I needed him; if only for my mother's sake I needed him. He represented a connection between our house and Elisabeth. In the long run, I couldn't stand between two women, or even three if one included Professor Szatmary. Ever since Herr von Stettenheim had so surprisingly found favour with my mother, Elisabeth sometimes came to our house. My mother had merely intimated that she didn't want to see Jolanth. Who, incidentally, was slowly distancing herself from Elisabeth. That too was partly to the credit of Herr von Stettenheim, and was another reason for me to be impressed with him. I got used to his unexpected manners (I found them less alarming, over time), his speech which was always two or three shades noisier than the room required. It was as though he didn't understand that rooms came in different shapes and sizes, a sitting room and a station hall, for instance.

In my mother's drawing room, he spoke with that rather too hasty voice that simple people fall into on the telephone. On the street he frankly shouted. And since everything he said was invariably vapid, it sounded twice as loud. For a long time I was surprised that my mother, who could be caused physical pain by a loud voice, a needless sound, any display of street music or parades, was able to tolerate and even take enjoyment in the voice of Herr von Stettenheim. It was only a couple of months later that by chance I was able to find out why this was.

One evening, I returned home unexpectedly. I wanted to say hello to my mother, and let her know I was back. The maid said she was in the library. The door of our library, which opened off the drawing room, was ajar so that I didn't have to knock. Evidently the old lady didn't hear my initial greeting. I supposed at first she had fallen asleep over her book. She was sitting facing the window, with her back to me. I came nearer, she wasn't asleep, she was reading and even turned a page just as I approached. 'Good evening, Mama!' I said. She didn't look up. I touched her. She jumped. 'Where have you sprung from?' she asked. 'Just passing by, Mama. I wanted to get Stiasny's address.' 'I haven't heard from him for a long time, I think he must have died.' Dr Stiasny was a police surgeon, the same age as me; my mother must have misunderstood. 'I mean that Stiasny,' I said. 'Yes, of course. I think he's been dead for two years now. He was over eighty.' 'Dead. I see,' I repeated, and I was forced to realise that my mother was deaf. It was only thanks to her discipline, that unusual discipline that we, her juniors, had been excused from birth, that she achieved the extraordinary strength to suppress her infirmity during those hours when she was expecting me back, me and others. During her long hours of waiting, she was readying herself to hear. She must certainly know that age had struck her one of the blows it likes to deal out. Soon – so I thought – she will be quite deaf, like the piano without strings! Yes, perhaps even that occasion, when in a fit of confusion she had asked for the strings to be taken out, even that had been a sense of her approaching deafness alive in her, and a vague fear that before long she wouldn't be able to hear notes any more! Of all the blows that old age has to give, this for my mother, a true child of music, must have been the worst. At that instant she attained for me an almost preternatural grandeur, moved into a different century, the epoch of a long-gone heroical nobility. Because to conceal and to deny frailty can only be heroic.

And so it was that she came to appreciate Herr von Stetten-heim. Obviously she found it easy to understand him, and so she was grateful to him. His banalities didn't exhaust her. I said goodbye; I wanted to go to my room to find Stiasny's address. 'Can I come at eight, Mama?' I called out, raising my voice a little. It was a little too much. 'No need to shout!' she said. 'Do come. We're having cherry dumplings, even though the flour is maize.'

I tried desperately to dismiss the thought of a boarding house. My mother running a B&B! What a truly absurd idea! Her deafness added to her dignity. Now perhaps she couldn't even hear the knocking of her own stick or her own footfall. I understood what made her so kind to our blond, heavy-set, rather slow-witted maid, who was apt to crash about, a good dull child from the suburbs. My mother and house-guests! Our house with innumerable bells, dinning into my ears already, the more my mother was unable to hear their impertinence. I had (so to speak) to hear for both of us, and feel offence for both of us too. But what other solution was there? Dr Kiniower was right. The arts and crafts swallowed one mortgage after another.

My mother didn't pay any attention to it. So I was left, as they say, with the responsibility. I and – responsible! Not that I was a coward, you understand. No, I was just not up to it. I wasn't afraid of death, but such things as offices, notaries and officials alarmed me. I couldn't count, it was all I could do to add. Multiplication made my head reel. So – yes. Me and responsibility!

In the meantime, Herr von Stettenheim was living his happy-go-lucky life, a ponderous bird. He always had money, he never had to borrow; on the contrary he treated all my friends. Of course we disliked him just the same. We suddenly fell silent when he wandered into the café. Moreover, he was in the habit of turning up with a different woman every week. He picked them up all over the place: dancers, checkout girls, seamstresses, milliners, cooks. He went on jaunts, he bought suits, he played tennis, he rode out in the Prater. One night I ran into him in our gateway on my way home. He seemed to be in a hurry, the car was waiting for him. 'I have to go!' he said, and threw himself into the car.

Elisabeth was sitting with my mother. She must have come

with Herr von Stettenheim. I sensed something different in our rooms, like an unusual, strange smell. Something unexpected must have taken place while I was gone. The two women were talking together when I walked in, but it was a sort of forced conversation, and I could tell its only purpose was to mislead me.

'I ran into Herr von Stettenheim in our gateway just now,' I began. 'Yes,' said Elisabeth, 'he gave me a lift. He was just here for ten minutes.' 'He's worried, poor fellow!' said my mother. 'Does he need money?' I asked. 'That's just it!' replied Elisabeth. 'There was a scene in the workshop today! Not to beat about the bush: Jolanth asked for money. We had to give her some. It's the first time she's asked for money. She's getting a divorce, you see. Stettenheim needs money urgently. My father has some bills due in the next few days, he says. I came here with Stettenheim.' 'Did my mother give him money?' 'Yes!' 'Cash?' 'A cheque!' 'What amount?' 'Ten thousand!'

I knew that my mother had just fifty thousand crowns left in Ephrussi's Bank, where they were gradually losing what was left of their value, according to the 'Jew's' report.

I began to pace up and down the room, as I had never dared to do before, in front of the stern and alarmed eyes of my mother. For the first time in my life I raised my voice in her presence, almost to a shout. At any rate, I was vehement. My whole accumulated anger with Stettenheim, with Jolanth, with my father-in-law overwhelmed me; and also my anger with my own weak nature. Anger with my mother was involved as well, jealousy of Stettenheim. For the first time in my mother's presence I dared to use an expression that was not acceptable outside officers' messes: 'Prussian swine.' It gave me quite a fright.

I allowed myself another liberty: I forbade my mother to issue cheques without my approval. In the same breath, I forbade Elisabeth to introduce anyone in need of money to my poor mother; any Tom, Dick or Harry was the expression I used. And since I knew myself, and knew very well that it was only once in a blue moon that I would express my will, my revulsion, yes, even my honest opinion of people, I deliberately worked myself into a deeper rage. I yelled: 'And I don't want to see the Professor ever again!' And: 'I've had it up to here with arts and crafts. I'm going to set things straight, Elisabeth! You're moving in here with me.'

My mother looked at me with her big sad eyes. It was obvious that she was equally frightened and delighted at my sudden outburst. 'His father was just the same,' she remarked to Elisabeth. Today, I even think it was possible that my father was speaking through me. I felt an impulse to stalk out of the house right away.

'His father', my mother continued, 'was a force of nature. He broke so many plates! So many plates when he was in a temper!' She spread out both arms to give Elisabeth a suggestion as to how many plates my father broke. 'Every six months!' my mother said. 'It was an illness, especially when we were packing our suitcases for Bad Ischl. He never liked that. My boy neither,' she added, even though she had never seen me do anything when we were packing.

I felt like taking her in my arms, the poor, deaf old lady. It was just as well she no longer heard the noises of the present time. She could hear those of the past, the smashed plates of my irascible father, for instance. She was also beginning to lose her memory, as is apt to happen with older persons who are hard of hearing. And that too was just as well! How kindly nature is! The infirmities it bestows upon age are actually a mercy. It gives us forgetfulness, deafness and dimmed eyesight when we are old; a little confusion too, shortly before death. The shadows it sends ahead of it are cool and beneficent.

# XXIX

Like many others of his sort, my father-in-law had bet on the fall of the French franc. It was a bad bet. Of all those 'many irons in the fire,' he was left with not one. The 'Jolan-Workshops' didn't bring in any money either. The lemon yellow furniture stayed on the shelf. The designs of Professor Jolanth Szatmary were hopeless. My wife Elisabeth's incomprehensible sketches were worth nothing.

My spry father-in-law lost his interest in arts and crafts. All of a sudden, he turned towards the newspaper industry. The press, people began to say in Austria, following the German usage. He took a share in the so-called Monday paper. There too he wanted to take me 'on board'. He was a tipster. He made money on it. Our house, once we had deducted the mortgages, had lost two-thirds of its value. And when the new currency was introduced, it turned out that my mother's savings in Ephrussi's Bank were barely worth a couple of thousand schillings.

The first person to disappear out of our world was Herr von Stettenheim. He 'made a break for it', one of those phrases he was so given to using. He didn't even write a goodbye letter. He just wired: 'Urgent rendezvous elsewhere. Will be back! Stettenheim.' Professor Jolanth Szatmary held on for longest. For weeks now, the auspicious premises with the lemon yellow furniture had been let to a firm called Iraq Ltd, which imported Persian carpets. For weeks now, my father-in-law had been negotiating the sale of his house to the city of Vienna. The world was changing fast, but Frau Jolanth Szatmary remained where she had always been: in the Regina Hotel. She was determined not to give up any of her habits, customs or usages. She was still designing. Her divorce had gone through: her ex-husband was sending her monthly cheques. She talked about going to San Francisco. Foreign parts appealed to her, Europe in her view was 'a mess'. But she didn't leave. She didn't quit. She appeared to me sometimes in nightmares. I saw her as a kind of infernal female, set on destroying my life and Elisabeth's. Why did she stay? Why was she still designing? Why did Elisabeth go to see her every day? To her hotel, to pick up perfectly redundant never-to-be-realized sketches?

'I feel I'm stuck,' Elisabeth confessed to me one day. 'I love you!' she said. 'But that woman won't let me go, I don't know what her game is.' 'Let's talk to my Mama!' I said. We went together to my house, to our house.

It was already late but my mother was still up. 'Mama,' I said, 'I've brought Elisabeth.' 'Good!' said my mother, 'so long as she stays!'

For the first time I slept with Elisabeth in my room, under our roof. It was as though my father's house heightened our love, blessed it. I will always remember that night, a true bridal night, the only bridal night of my life. 'I want your baby,' said Elisabeth, already half-asleep. I took it to be an expression of devotion. But in the morning, when she awoke – and she was always the first to wake – she embraced me, and there was a calm, almost a coldness to her voice when she said: 'I am your wife. I want to be pregnant by you. I want to finish with Jolanth, she disgusts me, I want a baby.'

From that morning on, Elisabeth stayed in our house. Professor Jolanth Szatmary sent a short farewell note. She wasn't going to San Francisco, as she had threatened to, she was going to Budapest, where she quite possibly belonged. 'What's Professor Keczkemet doing with herself?' my mother asked from time to time. 'She's in Budapest, Mama!' 'She'll be back!' predicted my mother. She would prove to be correct.

Now we were all living in one house, and it was going pretty well. My mother even did me the kindness of dropping her spiteful expressions. She no longer spoke about 'the Jew', but of Dr Kiniower, as she had for years previously. He was adamant that we should open a boarding house. He was one of those so-called practical people, who are unable to give up a so-called good idea, even if the people to whom he entrusts its execution are wholly unequal to such a task. He was a realist, which means he was as incorrigible as any fantast. He was incapable of seeing anything beyond a certain project's usefulness; and he lived in the conviction that all people, regardless of their nature, are equally able to carry out useful projects. It was as if a tailor were instructed to start making furniture, and without being told the dimensions of the houses, the rooms, the doors. And so we opened a boarding house. With the enthusiasm which an obsessive brings to the execution of his patented ideas, Dr Kiniower set about obtaining the licence we needed to go into business. 'You have so many friends!' he said to me. 'You have in all twelve rooms you can let. Your mother will be left with two. You and your wife will have four. All you need is a maid, a telephone, eight beds and bells.' And before we knew where we were, he was bringing in maid, telephone, engineers, beds. Then it was a matter of finding lodgers. Chojnicki, Stejskal, Halasz, Grünberger, Dvorak, Szechenyi, Hallersberg, Lichtenthal, Strohhofer: the lot of them were in a manner of speaking homeless. I introduced them all to our boarding house. The only one who paid in advance was Baron Hallersberg. Son of a wealthy Moravian sugar manufacturer, he espoused the expensive (and in our circle rather rare) habit of punctuality. He neither borrowed nor lent money. Impeccably brushed and pressed and correct, he lived with us and in our midst, tolerated on account of his gentleness, his discretion and his perfect lack of irony. 'The factory's going through hard times,' he would tell us, for instance. And straightaway, with paper and pencil, he would calculate his father's financial position. He expected us to look worried for him, and we obliged. 'I need to tighten my belt,' he would then say.

Well, in our boarding house, he tightened his belt. He paid punctually and in advance. He was afraid of debts and bills –

they 'add up,' he would say – and he took a dim view of the rest of us, because we let them 'add up'. At the same time he envied us for being able to let things 'add up'. The past master of this was Chojnicki. Accordingly, he was the one Hallersberg envied the most.

To my surprise, my mother was thrilled with our 'boarding house'. The sight of workmen in blue overalls crawling through our rooms obviously cheered her, and hearing the bells go, and lots of loud, cheerful voices. Obviously she saw this as a new life, and she was pleased to begin all over again. With a brisk step and a blithe cane she walked through the rooms, up and down the three floors of our house. Her voice was loud and cheerful. I had never seen or heard her like this.

At night, she sometimes dropped off in her chair. Her stick, like a trusty dog, lay at her feet.

But the 'boarding house', as Kiniower liked to say, was 'up and running'.

# XXX

I now slept in our house at the side of my wife. It soon turned out that she was blessed with an exceptional sense of so-called domesticity. She was positively obsessed, as many women are, with organization and cleanliness. Related to this fateful inclination was her jealousy. For the first time in my life I understood why women love their houses and flats more than they love their husbands. They are readying nests for their offspring. With unconscious cunning, they enmesh a man in a hopeless tangle of daily duties from which he has no hope of escaping. So there I was, sleeping in our house, at the side of my wife. It was my house. She was my wife. Indeed! Bed becomes like a second, discreet house in the middle of the public and plainly visible house, and the woman who awaits us there is loved, simply because she is there and available. She is there and available at any time we happen to return home. Therefore we love her. We love what is certain and safe. And if she waits up for us patiently, why, then we love her even more.

We now had about a dozen telephones in our house, and a dozen bells. Half a dozen men in blue overalls were at work on our water pipes. Dr Kiniower advanced us the money to pay for the improvements and rebuilding work. For my mother, he wasn't the Jew any more. He had been promoted to the rank of 'good fellow'.

In autumn we had an unexpected visitor: my cousin Joseph Branco. He arrived one morning, just like the very first time, and as though nothing had happened since then; as though we hadn't been through a World War; as though he and Manes Reisiger and I hadn't been prisoners of war, and then with Baranovich, and then in the camp; as though our country hadn't fallen to pieces; that was how he came to us, my cousin, the chestnut-roaster, with his chestnuts and his mule, brown of visage, black of hair and moustache, and for all that glowing golden like a sun, like every other year and as though nothing had happened, so Joseph Branco came to us, to sell his chestnuts. His son was healthy and quick-witted. He was going to school in Dubrovnik. His sister was happily married. His brother-in-law had managed to survive the War. They had two children between them, both boys, and for simplicity's sake both were called Branco.

And what had become of Manes Reisiger, I asked. 'Well, that's a long story,' my cousin Joseph Branco replied. 'He's waiting downstairs, he didn't want to come up.'

I ran downstairs to get him. I didn't recognize him right away.

He had a wild tangle of grey beard, like a personification of winter in children's storybooks. Why hadn't he come up, I asked him. 'For a year, Lieutenant,' he replied, 'I wanted to visit you. I was in Poland, in Zlotogrod. I wanted to be the cabbie Manes Reisiger again. But what is the world, what is a town, what is a man, what is a cabbie come to that, against God? God confused the world and he destroyed the little town of Zlotogrod. Crocuses and daisies grow where once our houses stood, and my wife is dead as well. A shell tore her in pieces, along with other inhabitants of Zlotogrod. So I went back to Vienna. At least I have my son Ephraim here.' Of course! His son Ephraim! I remembered the prodigy, and how Chojnicki had got him a place in the Music Academy. 'What's he doing now?' I asked Manes the cabbie.

'My Ephraim is a genius!' replied the old cabbie. 'He no longer plays. He doesn't need to, he says. He is a Communist, the editor of the "Red Flag." He writes splendid articles. Here they are.'

We went into my room. The cabbie Manes had all the articles of his brilliant son Ephraim in his pocket, quite a sizeable pile. He demanded that I read them aloud to him. I read them one after the other, in a loud voice. Elisabeth came out of her room; later on, as usual in the afternoons, all our residents gathered in my room, my friends. 'I'm not allowed to remain in Vienna,' said Manes Reisiger. 'I've been given an eviction order.' His beard bristled, his face shone. 'But my son Ephraim got me a false passport. Here it is.' And with that he showed us his false Austrian passport, combed his beard with his fingers, and said: 'Illegal!' and looked proudly at us.

'My son Ephraim', he began again, 'no longer needs to play. When the revolution comes, he will be a cabinet minister.'

He was as convinced of the coming of the world revolution as of the fact that in calendars Sunday is printed in red.

'This year the chestnuts have been poor,' said my cousin Joseph Branco. 'Many are wormy as well. I sell more apples now than I do chestnuts.'

'How did you manage to escape?' I asked.

'With God's help!' replied the cabbie Manes Reisiger. 'We were lucky enough to kill a Russian corporal. Joseph Branco tripped him up, and beat his brains out with a rock. Then I put on his uniform, took his rifle, and escorted Joseph Branco to Shmerinka. There we met the army of occupation. Branco joined up right away. He fought as well. I stayed with a good Jew, in civilian clothes. Branco had the address. As soon as the war was over, he came to me.'

'Splendid army!' cried Chojnicki, stepping into the room, to drink coffee with me, as he did every day. 'And what's your son Ephraim, the musician, doing?'

'He doesn't need music any more,' replied Manes Reisiger, the cabbie. 'He's making revolution.'

'We already have a few of that sort,' said Chojnicki. 'Not that you should imagine I'm in any way unsympathetic! But there's something wrong with the revolutions of today. They don't succeed. Your son Ephraim might have done better to stick to music.'

'You need a separate visa for each country now!' said my cousin Joseph Branco. 'I've never seen the like in all my born days. Each year I was able to go and sell my roast chestnuts wherever I felt like: in Bohemia, Moravia, Silesia, Galicia . . .', he listed all the lost Crown Lands. 'And now they're all off limits. Even though I have a passport. With a picture.' He took his passport out of his jacket pocket, and it went the rounds of everyone.

'He's just a chestnut-roaster,' said Chojnicki, 'but if you think about it, there is no more symbolic profession. Symbolic of the old Monarchy. This gentleman was able to sell his chestnuts all over, in half of Europe, you might say. Wherever people ate his roast chestnuts was Austria, and Franz Joseph was Emperor there. Now chestnuts require a visa! What a world! What am I doing in your b. and b. I should be with my brother in Steinhof!'

My mother came along, we heard her hard tread on the stairs. She dignified us with a visit every day at five o'clock. So far not one of our boarders had paid any money. Once Chojnicki, and once Szechenyi had shyly attempted to ask for their bill. Thereupon my mother had said that the caretaker was responsible for making out bills. But that wasn't true. In fact it was Elisabeth's job. She would take money from one or other of our guests, when the opportunity presented itself, and when the opportunity presented itself, she also paid our expenses. The bells shrilled all day long. We had two maids now. They ran up and down three flights of stairs like a couple of weasels. We enjoyed credit in the whole quarter. My mother was happy about the bells which she was still able to hear, the noise made by our guests, and the credit her house enjoyed. She didn't know, the poor old soul, that it was no longer her house. She believed it was hers because silence would fall in our rooms when she came down, with her white hair and black stick. Today she recognized Joseph Branco, and she greeted Manes Reisiger as well. Altogether, since we had opened our boarding house, she had become a little gregarious. She would have welcomed a lot of complete strangers. Only, she was getting increasingly deaf, and it seemed her infirmity was also affecting her reason – not because she was so tormented by it, but because she insisted on pretending it didn't exist, and on denying it.

# XXXI

In April of the following year, Elisabeth had her baby. She didn't give birth to it in hospital, but, as my mother demanded and insisted, at home.

I had fathered the child, demanded it, ordered it, insisted on it. Elisabeth had wanted it. I was in love with Elisabeth at that time, and was therefore jealous. I couldn't – as I imagined – expunge Professor Jolanth Szatmary from Elisabeth's memory, or in another way remove her, except by giving her a baby: the visible proof of my superior power. Professor Jolanth Szatmary was forgotten and expunged. But I too, old Trotta, was half-forgotten and half-expunged.

I was no longer Trotta, I was the father of my son. I had him baptized Franz Joseph Eugen.

It would be true to say that I changed completely from the moment my son was born. Chojnicki and all the friends who lived in our boarding house were waiting for me in my room on the ground floor, as excited as though they were to become fathers themselves. At four in the morning, the child was born. My mother brought me the news.

There was my son, a blood-red ugly creature, with far too big a head and flipper-like limbs. The creature cried all the time. It was the fruit of my loins, and I instantly fell in love with it, I even fell for the easy pride that I had sired a son and not a daughter. Yes, to get a better view of it, I even bent down over his tiny penis, which looked like a negligible red comma. No question: this was my son. No question: I was his father.

There have been millions and billions of fathers since the beginning of the world. Among these billions I now duly took my place. But from the moment I held my son in my arms, I experienced a dim version of that incomprehensibly lofty satisfaction that the Creator of the world must have felt when he saw his incomplete work nevertheless as done. When I held the tiny, bawling, ugly, scarlet thing in my arms, I could clearly feel what a change was taking place in me. However small and ugly and scarlet the thing in my arms: he still radiated an inexpressible strength. Or more: it was as though that soft, pathetic little body was a repository of all my strength, as though I was holding myself in my hands, and the best of myself at that.

The maternal quality of women is boundless. My mother reacted to her new grandson as though she had borne him herself, and the rest of whatever love she still had in her went to Elisabeth. It was only once she had a son from me, from my loins, that she accepted her as a daughter. In reality, Elisabeth was never more than the mother of her grandson.

It was as though she had only been waiting for this grandson to prepare for her own death. She started slowly to die, as she had all her life been slow. One afternoon she no longer came down to our room on the ground floor. One of the maids announced my mother had a headache. It wasn't a headache: my mother had had a stroke. She was left half-paralysed.

Over the years she remained a dearly loved, tenderly cared-for burden. I rejoiced each morning to see her still alive. She was an old lady, how easily she might die!

My son, her grandson, was brought to her every day. All she could do was blurt, 'Li'l fellow!' Her right side was paralysed.

# XXXII

To me my mother was a tenderly cared-for, dearly loved burden. I, who all my life, had never been drawn to any calling, now found myself suddenly with two: I was a son, and I was a father. I sat at my mother's bedside for hours on end. We had to take on a male nurse, the old lady was heavy. She had to be carried into the dining room every day, to table. Even sitting her down was a job. Sometimes she would ask me to wheel her through the rooms. She wanted to see and hear. Ever since she had become an invalid, she had the feeling she was missing out on a lot, really on everything. Her right eye drooped. When she parted her lips, it was as though she had an iron bracket clamped round the right half of her mouth. She could manage no more than the odd word at a time, usually nouns. Sometimes it almost seemed as if she was hoarding her vocabulary.

Straight after leaving my mother, I went into the room of my son. Elisabeth, who had been a devoted mother during the first few months, was slowly distancing herself from our son. I had given him the name Franz Joseph Eugen, among ourselves we called him Geni. Elisabeth started to leave the house frequently and for no reason. I didn't know where she was going, and I didn't ask her. She went, let her go! I even enjoyed being on my own without her, just me and my son. 'Geni!' I would call out, and his round, brown face would light up. I became more and more possessive of him. Not content with having sired him, ideally I would have been pregnant with him as well, and given birth to him. He crawled through our rooms, as swift as a weasel. He was already a human being – and still an animal and still an angel. I could see him changing by the day – if not by the hour. His brown curls grew thicker, the look in his large pale grey eyes was steadier, his eyelashes blacker and denser, the little hands themselves seemed to acquire a face, his little fingers grew strong and slender. His lips moved more eagerly, and his little tongue burbled more rapidly and meaningfully. I saw his first teeth appear, I saw Geni's first conscious smile, I was there on the day he took his first steps, towards the window, the light, the sun, with a sudden burst as though of inspiration; it was more like a brainwave than a physiological action. God Himself had given him the idea that man could walk on two feet. And lo and behold: my boy was walking on two feet.

For a long time I remained ignorant of where Elisabeth spent hours and sometimes whole days. She would talk of a friend, a seamstress, a bridge club. Our boarders, Hallersberg apart, paid infrequently and inadequately. When Chojnicki once in a blue moon received money from Poland, he would straightaway pay the rent for three or four boarders. Our credit in the area was unlimited. I didn't understand bills, and Elisabeth claimed to be keeping accounts. But one day, while she was gone, the butcher, the baker, the coffee merchant came to me, asking to be paid. I only had my allowance; every day before she went out Elisabeth left me some spare change. Sometimes we didn't see each other for days on end. I went to the Café Wimmerl with my friends. Among Chojnicki's duties was reading the newspaper, and giving lectures on politics. Every Sunday he went out to Steinhof, to visit his insane brother. He would talk to him about politics. Chojnicki would tell us: 'In general, my brother is barking mad, but where politics are concerned no one is as wise as he is. Today, for instance, he said to me, "Austria isn't a state, or a homeland, or a nation. It's a religion. The clerics and the clerical idiots who are governing us now, are making a so-called nation of us; of *us*, a supra-nation, the only supra-nation the world has ever seen." Another time he laid his hand on my shoulder, and said, "We are Polish, apparently, and always were. Why shouldn't we be? And we are Austrians too: why not? But there is a special idiocy of nationalists. The Social Democrats, who are the repulsive inventors of so-called nationalities, were the first to claim that Austria belongs to the German Republic. Now the cretinous Christian parties are taking their lead from the Social Democrats. The mountains always were the home of stupidity, so say I, Josef Chojnicki." And to maintain', Chojnicki continued, 'that such a man is deranged! I am convinced: he isn't in the least bit deranged. But for the end of the Monarchy, he wouldn't have become unhinged!' and so he ended his oration. No one spoke after such speeches. A heavy silence settled over our table, it didn't come from within us, it came from above. We didn't bewail our lost fatherland, we kept a respectful silence for it. Then sometimes, without any prior signal, we would start to sing old Army songs. We were all present and correct. But in reality we were all dead.

One day I accompanied Chojnicki on his weekly visit to his brother in Steinhof. The mad Chojnicki went walking in the courtyard; he lived in the locked ward, even though he showed no inclination to violence at all. He didn't recognize his brother. But when I told him my name, Trotta, he was straightaway lucid. 'Trotta,' he said. 'His father was here a week ago. The old District Commissioner Trotta. My friend, Lieutenant Trotta, lost his life at Krasne-Busk. Well, you are all dear to my heart! All you Trottas are.' And he embraced me. 'My address is Steinhof,' he continued. 'Since I moved here, it has become the capital city and residence of Austria. I keep the crown here. I am authorized to do so. My uncle Ledochovsky used to say: that little Josef will one day be a great man. Now I am. He was right.'

Chojnicki was now talking nonsense. He called for his socks. When he was confined to the asylum, he became an enthusiastic knitter. 'I am knitting the Monarchy,' he would say from time to time. When I tried to take my leave, he said: 'I don't have the honour of knowing you.' 'My name is Trotta,' I said. 'Trotta', he replied, 'was the Hero of Solferino. He saved the life of the Emperor Franz Joseph. That Trotta is long dead. It seems to me, sir, that you are a deceiver.'

It was on that same day that I learned what kept my wife away from home so often and for such long periods, why she left our boy alone, and my poor crippled mother. When I got home, I ran into the only two people in the world I really hated: Professor Jolanth Szatmary and Kurt von Stettenheim.

It turned out that they had been back in Vienna for ages. It turned out that they had abandoned arts and crafts. They were now utterly devoted to the cinema. Alexander Rabinovich – 'the renowned Alexander Rabinovich, have you not heard of him?' thus Herr von Stettenheim – had started a 'production company' in Vienna; another company! It turned out that Elisabeth had no intention of remaining a mother, no, she was dead set on becoming an actress. Film was calling her, and she felt a calling to go into film.

One day she disappeared, leaving me the following note:

Dear husband, your mother hates me, and you don't
love me either. I feel a calling. I will go with Jolanth and
Stettenheim. Forgive me. The call of art is powerful.
Elisabeth.

I showed this note to my crippled mother. She read it twice over. Then she took my head in her still hale left hand, and said: 'Boy! B–b–boy!' she said. It was as though she was congratulating me and pitying me, both.

Who can say what clever things she might have said, if she hadn't been paralysed.

My son no longer had a mother. The mother of my son was an actress in Hollywood. The grandmother of my son was an old crippled woman.

She died in February.

## XXXIII

My mother died during the first days of February. She died as she had lived, quietly and aristocratically. To the priest who had come to give her the last rites, she said: 'Please hurry, Your Reverence! God doesn't have as much time as the church sometimes likes to imagine.' The priest was accordingly quick about it. Then my mother called for me. She was no longer babbling. She spoke fluently, as before, as if her tongue had never been paralysed. 'If you should ever see Elisabeth again,' she said to me, 'I don't think it's very likely, but tell her if you do that I never cared for her. I am dying now, but I don't think much of those devout individuals who even on their deathbeds are still lying and come over all magnanimous. Now bring me your son, so that I can see him once more.'

I went downstairs, I picked up my son, who was big and already quite a weight; I was happy that he was so solid as I carried him up the stairs. My mother hugged him and kissed him, and gave him back to me.

'Send him away,' she said, 'far away! He's not to grow up here. Go away now!' she added, 'I want to die by myself.'

She died that same night, it was the night of the Revolution. Shots rang out through the city, and Chojnicki told us over dinner that the government was shooting at the workers. 'Dollfuss', thus Chojnicki, 'wants to kill the proletariat. God forgive me, I really can't stand him. He is digging his own grave. The world has never seen the like . . . !'

When my mother was buried, in the Central Cemetery, Second Gate, there was still shooting throughout the city. All my friends – which is to say, all our lodgers – accompanied my mother and me. It was hailing, just as it was on the night of my return from the War. It was the same vicious stony hail.

We buried my mother at ten in the morning.

When we emerged from the Second Gate of the Central Cemetery, I saw Manes Reisiger. He was following a coffin, and I went with him, without a word. The coffin was taken to the Third Gate, to the Jewish section.

I stood over the open grave. After the Rabbi had spoken the prayer, Manes Reisiger stepped up and said: 'The Lord hath given him, the Lord hath taken him away, praised be His Name in all eternity. The Cabinet Minister has shed blood, and his blood, too, shall be shed. It shall flow like a rushing torrent.' People tried to restrain Manes Reisiger, but he carried on in a strong voice: 'Whoever lives by the sword', he said, 'shall die by the sword. God is great and just.' And then he broke down. We took him aside, while his gifted son Ephraim was buried. He was a rebel, he had taken up arms and been killed.

Joseph Branco still came to our house occasionally. His chestnuts were now his only interest in life. They were mouldy this year and wormy, and he, Joseph Branco, could only sell roasted apples.

I sold the house. I kept the bed and breakfast.

It was as though the death of my mother had driven all my friends out of our house. They moved away, one after the other. We met in the Café Wimmerl.

Only my son was still alive for me. 'Whoever kills,' said Manes Reisiger, 'shall be killed.'

I had no more interest in the world. I sent my son away to my friend Laveraville in Paris.

I was alone, alone, alone.

I went to the Kapuzinergruft.

# XXXIV

That Friday too I was waiting for evening to fall. It was only in my dearly loved evenings that I still felt at home, since I no longer had a house and a home. I waited, as usual, to commit myself into its care, which was kindlier in Vienna than the silence of the nights once the cafés have shut, once the lamp posts are tired, worn out from their pointless illumination. They longed for the tardy morning, and their own extinction. Yes, they were tired, the insomniac streetlights, they waited for morning, so that they could sleep.

Oh, I remembered how they had silvered the nights of my youth, the kindly sons and daughters of the heavens, suns and stars that had agreed to come down to light the city of Vienna. The skirts of the girls on the game in Kärntnerstrasse still went down to their ankles. When it rained, the sweet creatures picked them up, and I saw their exciting button-boots. Then I went to Sacher's to see my friend Sternberg. He was sitting in a corner, always the same one, and he was always the last one there. I picked him up. We meant to go home together, but we were young, and the night was young (although the hour was advanced), and the streetwalkers were young, especially the older ones, and the lanterns were young too ...

So we strolled through our own youth, and the youthful night. The houses we stayed in seemed to us like tombs, or at best shelters. The night watchmen saluted us, Count Sternberg gave them cigarettes. Often we patrolled with the constables through the pallid and deserted city centre, and sometimes one of the sweet creatures would walk with us, with a different walk to the one she had on her beat. At that time, the streetlights were rarer and more modest, but they shed a stronger light, and some of them even swayed in the wind ...

Later on, when I returned from the war, not just older, but positively antique, the Viennese nights were wrinkled and withered, like ancient drabs; evening didn't slip into night as it had once done, but avoided it, turned pale, and ran off as soon as it saw night coming. You had to grab these shy, fleeting evenings before they disappeared, and what I liked best was to catch them in the parks, the Volksgarten or the Prater, and then to savour the last sweetest lingering of them in a café, where they seeped in, gentle and mild, like a fragrance.

That evening too I went to the Café Lindhammer, and I conducted myself as though I was by no means as agitated as the other customers. For a long time now, ever since my return from the war, I had seen myself as someone who had no right to be alive. I had long since got used to viewing events that the newspapers blazoned as 'historic' with the piercing regard of one no longer of this world. I was on extended leave from death. Death could end my furlough at any moment. Of what interest to me were the things of this world? ...

Still, they preoccupied me, and especially they preoccupied me on that Friday. What was at issue was whether I, retired from life, could go on drawing my retirement pension, as hitherto, in an embittered tranquillity; or if that too, my poor embittered tranquillity, or the resignation I had got used to calling 'peace' was to be taken from me. Of late, whenever one or other of my friends came to tell me the time had come for me to take an interest in the fate of my country, I would say my usual piece: 'Leave me alone!' – but I knew that what I should have said was: 'Leave me to despair!' My sweet despair! It too is all gone. Gone the way of my unfulfilled desires and hopes ...

So I sat in the café and while my friends at my table still were talking about their personal lives, I, who had seen the elimination by a merciful and implacable fate of all possibility of personal life, had only the collective to commune with, which all my life had concerned me least, and which all my life I had sought to elude ...

It was weeks since I had last read a newspaper, and the conversation of my friends who seemed to live off newspapers, yes, to be kept alive by news and rumours, washed past me with no effect, like the waves of the Danube when I sometimes sat on the Franz-Josefs-Kai, or on the Elisabeth Promenade. I was switched off; switched off. To be switched off among the living means something like exterritorial. I was an exterritorial among the living.

And the agitation of my friends on that Friday evening struck me as unnecessary; until that instant when the café door was yanked open, and a young man stood in the doorway in unusual dress. He wore leather gaiters, a white shirt, and a sort of forage cap that looked to me like a cross between a bed-pan and our good old army caps, in a word, a sub-Prussian item of headgear. (Because on their heads the Prussians wear neither hats nor caps but headgear.) Remote from the world as I was, and the Hell that it represented to me, I was hardly likely to distinguish among the new caps and uniforms, much less to identify any of them. There were white, blue, green and red shirts; trousers in black, brown, green or sky blue; boots and spurs, leather and straps and belts and daggers in sheaths of all kinds. I at any rate had decided for myself long ago, when I returned from the War, that I was not going to interest myself in them any more, and not to learn any. And so I was initially more surprised than my friends at this person, who, to judge from his appearance, looked as though he might have come up from the toilets in the basement, and yet had walked in the street door. For a few seconds I actually thought the downstairs toilets, with which I was perfectly familiar, had been rehoused, and were now outside, and one of the men who worked there as attendants had just stepped in to let us know that they were all occupied. Instead the man said: 'Fellow countrymen! The government has fallen! A new German people's government has been established.'

Ever since I had returned from the World War to my reduced fatherland, I had not mustered a belief in any form of government; much less a people's government. Even now – shortly before what will in all probability be my final hour, I, a human being, dare to speak the truth – I belong to an evidently lost world, in which it was only to be expected that a people would be ruled in some form, and that, unless it were to cease being a people, it would not rule itself. To my deaf ears – which I have often heard described as 'reactionary' – it sounded as though a beloved woman had said to me she no longer needed me; she could sleep with herself, and was even obliged to, purely in order to contract a child.

I was therefore surprised by the shock that came over my friends at the sight of this jackbooted gentleman and his exotic announcement. Between the lot of us, we took up three tables. A moment later, I was all alone. I was all alone, it was as though I had been looking for myself and to my surprise suddenly found myself, alone. All my friends had got up from their chairs, and instead of bidding me 'Good night!' first, as had been their way for years, they called: 'Waiter, bill please!' But since our waiter Franz didn't appear, they called out to the Jewish café owner Adolf Feldmann: 'We'll pay tomorrow!' and they walked out, without looking at me.

I thought they meant it, that they really would return tomorrow to pay, and that Franz was just detained in the kitchen or somewhere, and hence unable to come promptly when called. But after ten minutes, the café owner Adolf Feldmann came out from behind the bar, in his hat and coat, and said: 'Baron, this is goodbye. If we should meet anywhere in the world, we will recognize each other. Tomorrow you surely will not come here. Not with the new German people's government. Will you go home, or do you think you will stay here?'

'I'll stay here, like every other night,' I replied.

'Then farewell, Baron! I'm turning out the lights. Here are two candles!'

And with that he lit a couple of pallid candles, and before I could account for my impression that he had left me two funeral candles, all the lights in the café went out, and pale, with a black top hat on his head, looking more like an undertaker than the jovial, silver-bearded Jew Adolf Feldmann, he handed me a massy lead swastika, and said:

'Just in case, Baron! Enjoy your schnapps in quiet! I'll let the shutters down. When you're ready to go, you can open them from inside. The pole is on the right of the door.'

'I'd like to pay,' I said.

'There's no time for that today!' he said.

And he was gone, and I heard the shutter clatter down outside the door.

So I was alone at the table, with the two candles. They stuck to the imitation marble tabletop and reminded me of white, upright, burning worms. At any instant I expected them to start to writhe in the manner of worms.

As I began to feel a little spooked, I called out: 'Franz, the bill!' as I did every other evening.

But in came not Franz the waiter, but the guard dog who was also called 'Franz', and whom I had never liked. He was a sandy yellow colour, and had rheumy eyes and a slimy muzzle. I don't care for animals, and I care even less for people who love animals. All my life it seemed to me that people who love animals withhold some of that love from people, and that view seemed particularly justified when I happened to hear that the Germans of the Third Reich love those German sheepdogs called Alsatians. 'Poor sheep!' I said to myself when I heard that.

And now the dog Franz came over to me. Although I was his enemy, he rubbed his face against my knee, as though to beg my forgiveness. And the candles burned, the funeral candles, my own funeral candles! No bells sounded from St Peter's church. As I never carry a watch on my person, I did not know how late it was.

'Franz, the bill please!' I said to the dog, and he climbed on to my lap.

I picked up a sugar lump and held it out to him.

He didn't take it. He just whimpered. And thereupon he licked my hand, the hand from which he had refused the gift of a piece of sugar.

Now I blew out one candle. I removed the other from the imitation marble tabletop, and went to the door, and with the pole pushed up the shutter from inside.

I wanted to escape the dog and his affection.

When I stepped out on to the pavement with the pole in my hand to lower the shutter, I saw that the dog Franz had not abandoned me. He was following me. He refused to stay. He was an old dog. He had worked for at least ten years in the Café Lindhammer, just as I had for the Emperor Franz Joseph; and now he could work no more. Now both of us could work no more. 'The bill, Franz!' I said to the dog. He whimpered in reply.

Day was breaking over the alien, occupying crosses. A dawn breeze shook the ancient lights which, in this street at least, had not yet been extinguished. I walked along the deserted streets with a strange dog. He was set on following me. Where would we go? I had as little idea as he did.

The Kapuzinergruft, where my Emperors lie buried in stone sarcophagi, was locked. The Capuchin brother came up to me, and asked me: 'What do you want?'

'I want to visit the tomb of my Emperor Franz Joseph,' I replied.

'May God bless you!' replied the monk, and he made the sign of the cross over me.

'Long live the Emperor!' I called.

'Ssh!' said the monk.

Where can I go now, I, a Trotta? . . .

# TRANSLATOR'S
# ACKNOWLEDGEMENTS

Some thanks are in order: to the founders and organizers of the *Spycherpreis*, the commune of Leuk and the canton of Wallis (especially Alex Hagen, Thomas Hettche, Carlo Schmidt and Hans Schnyder) for generously establishing me in a place where I have worked so happily for so many years; to Will Hobson – who improved my translation of *The Radetzky March* a decade ago (then it was synchronized page-turning over milky coffee, now – alas! – it is electronic ping-pong) – for kindly finding the time to help me with this sequel: it is a pleasure to be indebted again to his ear and resourcefulness and attention to detail; and to Philip Gwyn Jones, Bella Lacey, Aidan O'Neill and others at Granta for their noble commitment to this project; and to my friends Jana Marko and Peter Sokol for help and support.